Dear Romance Reader,

Welcome to a world of breathtaking passion and never-ending romance.

Welcome to *Precious Gem Romances*.

It is our pleasure to present *Precious Gem Romances*, a wonderful new line of romance books by some of America's best-loved authors. Let these thrilling historical and contemporary romances sweep you away to far-off times and places in stories that will dazzle your senses and melt your heart.

Sparkling with joy, laughter, and love, each *Precious Gem Romance* glows with all the passion and excitement you expect from the very best in romance. Offered at a great affordable price, these books are an irresistible value—and an essential addition to your romance collection. Tender love stories you will want to read again and again, *Precious Gem Romances* are books you will treasure forever.

Look for eight fabulous new *Precious Gem Romances* each month—available only at Wal★Mart.

Lynn Brown, Publisher

THE LADY AND THE COP

Shauna Michaels

Zebra Books
Kensington Publishing Corp.
http://www.zebrabooks.com

ZEBRA BOOKS are published by

Kensington Publishing Corp.
850 Third Avenue
New York, NY 10022

Copyright © 1996 by Margaret Daley

All rights reserved. No part of this book may be reproduced in any form or by any means without the prior written consent of the Publisher, excepting brief quotes used in reviews.

If you purchased this book without a cover you should be aware that this book is stolen property. It was reported as "unsold and destroyed" to the Publisher and neither the Author nor the Publisher has received any payment for this "stripped book."

Zebra and the Z logo Reg. U.S. Pat. & TM Off.

First Printing: November, 1996
10 9 8 7 6 5 4 3 2 1

Printed in the United States of America

To my husband, Mike
Thank you for all your love and for standing by me through thick and thin.
Without you this wouldn't be possible.

Chapter One

The wail of the siren pierced the air, drowning out the deafening sound the muffler was making. Tess Morgan looked back in the rearview mirror, swore softly, and eased up on the accelerator. Parking on the side of the road, she saw the motorists passing her and thought about taking her daughter's blankie and throwing it over her head to hide from their curious stares. The color in her cheeks reflected the red lights flashing behind her.

"Why me? Why now?" she muttered while she watched the policeman step from his car.

The officer strode toward her. His tall, beautifully proportioned frame struck her first, but that observation fled quickly to be replaced with a series of others—his fierce, commanding countenance; his casual way of moving that belied an alertness; his lean, whipcord strength evident by the muscles bunched beneath his short sleeve dark blue shirt; his aviator sunglasses that hid his eyes from her; his physical magnetism that kept her staring at him when common sense told her to do otherwise.

When he stopped briefly to write down her license plate number, a rush of expelled air stirred her bangs. This officer sent her heart pounding; she always did have a weakness for a man in a uniform. With each purposeful step that brought him closer, her pulse reacted until it sped through her veins at an alarming rate.

Forcing herself to look away, Tess trained her gaze on a dent on her hood and gripped her steering wheel. She was vividly aware when he came to a halt beside her and leaned down. His musk scented after-shave permeated the car. When she centered her gaze on the man looming in her window, she saw her reflection in his sunglasses, a wide-eyed look on her face. She tried to discern beneath the dark shades, to sense any softness under the hard, unyielding lines of his expression. She couldn't.

"Ma'am, may I see your driver's license?"

His question freed her from her trance. "Driver's license?"

"You do have one?" he asked, one eyebrow cocked.

Color flamed her cheeks even more. "I believe so. Somewhere."

She gave him a weak smile, then turned to rummage through her purse. She found her wallet and rifled through it. She didn't have her license. What did she do with it? Tension cramped her stomach. She certainly couldn't afford one ticket let alone two.

"I can't seem to find it. I know I have one. I just moved here and went and got an Oklahoma license last week. I had it in my pocket yesterday when I drove to the park to run."

"Maybe, ma'am, it's still there," he said in a dark, rough-edged voice that had a calming effect.

"No, I'm sure I put it in here when I got back home." Frustrated, her hands shaking, she dropped the contents of her oversized bag on the seat next to her. She moved aside the apple, the curling iron and the small stuffed bear while she continued, "Unless Katie played with my purse last night. Anything's possible with a curious four-year-old." She finally saw the license, grabbed it and held it up as though she had won an Oscar. "See, here it is."

"So it is." He took it from her. A slight smile cracked his stern expression.

Oh, Lord, after all that had happened to her this morning, she would have to act like a blithering idiot chattering nervously when she needed all her wits about her if she was going to talk this policeman out of a ticket which she couldn't afford. She could barely afford money for the gas to get her to her job interview.

After examining the piece of plastic, he looked back up into her face, nothing discernible in his expression. "Ms. Morgan, are you running late?"

She raked her hand through her short curls, nervous because all she saw was herself mirrored in his sunglasses. "No, just running fast."

His half smile became full-fledged, denting the slant of his high cheekbones. "You were going forty five miles *fast* which is fine on the highway but not on a city street with a speed limit of thirty five."

"I have a job interview this morning. The first promising one since I moved here last month. The market isn't great for computer programmers right now. Just my luck, Katie picked today to rebel on wearing what I had picked out for her. I've been choosing her clothes for the past four years. But not today. Then Wesley couldn't find his lunch box with Batman on it and Shaun *had* to have a certain kind of folder for school and it had to be today. I had to make a special trip to the store, then drop him off at school because he missed the bus. Why can't kids tell you these things the day before?"

"I've asked myself that very same question several times in the past month since school started."

"How many children do you have?"

"Two. One started first grade this year."

"I have a first grader, too. Also, a third grader and my curious four-year-old." She had him, Tess thought with an inner smile. There was a connection now between them. How could he give her a ticket when they had first graders in common? Just in case, she smiled openly at him. "How old is your other child, Officer," Tess looked at his name plate, "Smith."

"Eighteen months."

"Oh, I love that age. The terrible twos hasn't descended yet."

He looked at her with a disconcerting directness for a long moment before clearing his throat and replacing his smile with that stern, no-nonsense expression. "Mrs. Morgan, do you also realize your safety sticker is overdue?"

"Every time I drive this car. People can hear me coming five blocks away. I can't get my safety sticker because of my muffler and I can't get a muffler without a job and money. I promise I will the minute I land this job." She resisted the urge to glance at her watch. She didn't really need to be reminded the minutes were ticking away all too quickly.

"Where are you headed?"

"Carson International."

"When is your job interview?"

"Ten o'clock."

"Fifteen minutes. Well, then I'll make this quick for the sake of Cimarron City's noise level." He flipped open his black pad. "I'll give you a warning this time. Don't let me catch you speeding again, Mrs. Morgan." He scribbled on the paper, ripped it off and handed it to her. "Consider this a welcoming gift from the city."

"Thank you, Officer Smith." Tess stuffed the warning into her pocket.

He turned to leave, swung back around and added, "And get that muffler fixed. That's what attracted me to your car in the first place. You're right it's loud and can be heard blocks away. The next policeman might not be so welcoming."

Tess started the engine and wanted to cringe when she heard the offending piece of junk come to life. Not only did she need a new muffler but a whole new car. This one was on its last wheel. As she pulled out onto the street, she waved to the officer who was watching her from his vehicle.

Zachariah Smith laughed at the sight of Mrs. Morgan driving away. She would be lucky if she made it to Carson International. Not only did that car sound awful, but it looked like a demolition derby reject with its two-tone paint job—rust and blue.

Thinking about her car led his thoughts to the woman behind the wheel. Her hair was a bundle of curls, rich, dark with hints of wildfire in them. They framed her beautiful face like a halo of flames. Her soft voice was throatily sexy, even when she was chattering away, and she had a disarming smile that touched a part of him that he had thought was dead.

He flipped his pad open to the carbon copy of his warning. Tess Morgan. 513 Oakcrest Drive. That was four blocks from his house. Too bad all the good ones were married. She would have been interesting to get to know.

Tess stuck her hand into the pocket of her dress and withdrew the warning that Officer Smith had written earlier that day. She read what he had scribbled in a bold handwriting across the middle of the piece of paper, "Good luck with your job interview. Z. Smith." As she ran her fingertips over the letters, she wondered what the Z. stood for. It had to be an unusual first name to fit an unusual man.

Oh, well, she wouldn't see him again, she thought, shrugging and replacing the warning in her pocket.

Tess looked out the window over the kitchen sink, a smile playing about the corners of her mouth. She had done it. She had a job and a chance to provide for her children. Ever since meeting that nice Officer Smith today, her luck had changed. He had been her good luck charm.

A vision of her good luck charm popped into her thoughts, causing her breath to catch. The man looked dynamite in a uniform and his smile was pure sexy. A picture of him walking toward her earlier filled her mind with warm images. Her first impression of strength and power had only been reconfirmed when he had talked to her, his voice deep, husky, with a calm, reassuring tone. Tess thought about the man's two children and knew instinctively he would be a good father, a good provider.

Too bad he was married, she mused, then instantly banished that thought from her mind. She hadn't come to Cimarron City to get involved with anyone.

"Mommie, Wesley won't play marbles wif me," Katie said, then immediately stuck her thumb into her mouth.

Her daughter's declaration startled Tess from her daydream. Conscious of the patches of red on her cheeks that the vision of the policeman had produced, Tess glanced down at her daughter, who stood with that determined look on her face, and knew she would never make the Back to School Night on time. The story of her life, late for everything, Tess thought and wiped her hands on a towel next to the sink. She knelt in front of her youngest child. "He has to clean his room first."

"He promised to play after dinner."

"You'll just have to wait until he's through with his chore." Tess started to rise to finish her own chore when her daughter's pout warned her Katie wouldn't let this go.

"He promised."

"Go see if Shaun will. I think he's out back playing with Bruce."

Her daughter's face lit up, and she raced out of the

kitchen. Tess sighed and turned back to the dinner dishes. One disaster averted. But it would be a miracle if she could get out the door in the next thirty minutes without something else happening. Three children had a way of roughening the waters of life.

As she scrubbed a pan, Tess heard Bruce, their Great Dane, barking. She watched from the kitchen window while Katie dragged Shaun into the house, their dog none too happy to be left alone outside on the rope they had devised to keep him in the yard since there was no fence. Her eldest child wasn't too happy either, but Katie ruled her two brothers and they rarely denied her anything.

Tess let another sigh escape her lips and thought back over the day's events. She still couldn't believe she had the job, that her car had made it to Carson's and back home. After a long year of fighting uphill for everything, maybe things were going to start going her way now.

"I'll finish up in here," her grandmother said as she entered the kitchen.

Tess continued to wash the dishes, stacking them into the drain. "You can dry. With both of us working we'll be done in no time."

"But you have that meeting tonight. You'll be late."

"Why spoil a perfect record."

"That'll have to change with this new job."

Tess chuckled. "I've already set my alarm for an hour earlier in the morning. That should allow me enough time to settle any disputes that erupt here and get to Carson's by eight."

Granny Kime picked up the towel and a glass and began to dry. "It's about time something went your way. I can't stand to see you struggle since Brad left you."

The mention of her ex-husband's name sent a chill down Tess's spine. "It was for the best," she replied evenly while inside she quavered.

"Best?" Granny Kime shook her head. "How can you

say that? He walked out on you and left you with three young children. Have you forgotten what it has been like for you this past year?"

Tess drained the sink, staring at the soapy water swirling downward. "Forgotten? Never, Granny Kime." The pain she had felt when she had read Brad's note on his pillow resurfaced and pierced her heart. She had awakened one morning with hope that they could work their problems out, only to find his letter. He had written the brief note to tell her that he wanted a divorce and that he had moved out. He had left his family without a backward glance and she never wanted to feel that kind of betrayal again. "I don't need a man to make my life complete. I won't ever depend upon one again."

"Don't judge the rest of mankind by Brad."

Tess draped the dishcloth over the nozzle. "I'm not. It's just that I married Brad right out of high school. I went from the safety of your home to his. It's time to find out if I can do this on my own."

"You can. You're my granddaughter."

Tess laughed. "I could always count on you for support."

"Well, I'm glad you finally came to your senses and decided to move here. New Orleans is no place to raise three children all by yourself."

"Speaking of three children, it's awfully quiet. I'd better go check on them before I leave. I don't trust silence."

Tess walked through the living room, relieved to see Katie bent over the glass bowl full of black marbles, her little hands grabbing them to stuff into a plastic cup as fast as she could. Tess smiled at the game her daughter had made up to play with her brothers. Whoever filled the cup up the most was the winner and somehow she always managed to win.

Sticking her head into the bedroom Wesley and Shaun shared, Tess noticed her second child was playing with his Lego set, not putting it away. Taking a deep breath of the lavender laced air, Tess was glad she had placed some of the scent in the aroma pot. She needed its calming effect right about now. She pushed the door open wide and stood in the entrance with her hands on her hips. Wesley was so engrossed in what he was doing that he didn't hear her until she cleared her throat.

"Young man, what are you doing?"

He froze. "Playing."

"I can see that. Maybe I should rephrase my question. What are you supposed to be doing?"

"Cleaning up. But, Mom, I'm almost done. See this warship I'm making."

Tess let her gaze travel over the chaotic terrain of her son's room. It looked as if he had already staged a war of mass destruction. "You're not done in my book and that's the only one that matters."

"But, Mom, I've been working all evening."

"You have?" She again ran her gaze over the mess scattered everywhere on the floor. "If I'm not mistaken, somewhere under all this," she gestured at the disorder, "there is a brown carpet. I'd like to see it when I come back to check your progress."

"But I've got this great idea for this ship. I thought I deserved a break."

Tess glanced down at her watch, noting her time was running out. "You've been at it for twenty minutes. You get a break when it's done. Now if you don't want me to take the Lego set away, I would suggest you get this room cleaned up. You've got until I leave. Fifteen minutes." She closed the door on her son's third, "But, Mom," and left to change into something suitable for her first school meeting in a new town.

Tess opened the classroom door a few inches and peered inside. Mrs. Young, Wesley's first grade teacher, was speaking to the group of parents, all stuffed into their children's undersized chairs. For a brief moment Tess thought about sneaking back to Shaun's room and just skipping Wesley's. But her second child was having a problem adjusting to school, and she needed to be here.

Taking a deep, calming breath, she slipped into the room, hoping no one noticed that she was late. Even though she was as quiet as possible, she managed to bump into a chair and several heads turned to look at her. She smiled weakly and slid into the only available desk.

Mrs. Young paused for a few seconds, then resumed her speech about class procedures. Tess felt embarrassed and awkward, sitting in a chair two sizes too small for her.

"I see, Mrs. Morgan, you're running late again."

Tess whipped her head around and looked into Officer Smith's laughing gaze. If it had been humanly possible, she would have crawled under the chair and hid in that moment. Instead, she put her finger to her mouth to indicate being quiet, then tried to concentrate on what Mrs. Young was saying.

Tess really did try to listen, but all her mind would dwell on was the man sitting next to her. Wearing tan slacks and a black turtleneck shirt, she couldn't believe he could actually look even better than he did in his uniform. She could smell his after-shave lotion that had perfumed her car all the way to Carson's this morning, and her heart began to beat a shade faster.

The only reason she was attracted to this man was because he was married with two children. Safe. Someone whom she could fantasize about and that was all. Pleased with her self-analysis, she determinedly blocked the man's disturbing presence from her mind.

"Now, do any of you have any questions?" Mrs. Young asked the audience.

Tess had several but wasn't about to ask any because she had no idea what the woman had gone over in class before she had arrived. How was a parent supposed to split herself in two and be in both of her children's classes at the same time? It was moments like this that renewed her anger at her ex-husband for leaving her in this situation. He should be a part of his children's lives, but instead he had walked away, not acknowledging they even existed and certainly not paying child support.

"Lance tells me you want them to read every night to us. Is that all the homework they have?" Officer Smith asked Mrs. Young, bringing Tess's attention back to him.

"Yes, that's right. I'll start keeping a chart of what they read next month. Second semester the class will also have a weekly spelling test. Studying for that will be homework, too."

Homework? Wesley hadn't said anything about that. Tess tried to get him to read with her when she put him to bed, but he resisted. She had been so busy the past month with moving to Cimarron City and trying to find a job to support her family that she hadn't kept on top of things as she should have. She knew Wesley wasn't happy, but she was beginning to suspect the problem went deeper than needing time to adjust to a new town. Had she been so immersed in her own troubles that she hadn't seen the seriousness of Wesley's? She had thought time would heal her son's feelings of uncertainty since Brad had left. Maybe she was wrong.

"We'll be having parent conferences in two weeks. Don't forget to sign up before you leave if you haven't already. Please feel free to look around the room. We have work displayed on the walls and each student has a folder on his desk," Mrs. Young announced.

Realizing she was in her son's desk, Tess flipped open Wesley's folder and found only two papers inside, one of a drawing of their house in New Orleans and the other a story copied from the board. The letters were sloppy as if Wesley had raced through the assignment. She knew he could write better than this. Glancing about her, she noticed the other students had a lot more pieces for their parents to view.

Staring at her son's work, Tess tried not to get too upset over another problem developing. She had coped with so many in the past year; she could handle this, too. She had to because there was no one else for Wesley or her other children except her. She was determined to be the best mother and father for them.

"Did you get the job?"

Tess blinked, slowly focusing on Officer Smith. "Yes, as a matter of fact I did." Her gaze riveted to his eyes, gray with hints of silver in them.

"Then you weren't late?"

"Only a few minutes and they were running later."

She stretched out her hand toward the policeman. "My name is Tess Morgan and I want to thank you again for not giving me a ticket this morning."

He took her hand within his and shook it. "I'm Zachariah Smith and you're welcome."

His smile coupled with the warmth from his touch sent her heartbeat galloping. The look in his compelling gaze robbed her of breath. For a few seconds she was at a loss for words until he dropped his hand away from hers and she said the first thing that came into her mind, "Not only do we both have two first graders in common, but they're in the same class." She could get an A for her powers of deduction, she realized as she felt a blush stain her face.

"So they are."

His eyes like pieces of silver that had caught and held sunshine glinted with a smile. She would never understand why a man with such beautiful eyes would wear dark sunglasses to conceal them from the world. Definitely his best asset, Tess thought, suddenly realizing she was staring at him. She was doing a lot of that lately.

"Is your wife here tonight?" she asked and almost bit

her tongue for the question. She was becoming an expert at putting her foot in her mouth when it came to this man.

"My wife is dead."

"I'm sorry," Tess automatically murmured, deciding both feet were fitting nicely in her mouth.

"And Mr. Morgan? Is he in your third grader's class?"

"No, I have no earthly idea where Mr. Morgan is. We're divorced."

Zachariah's smile grew, making his eyes sparkle. "Well, now that we have all the important questions out of the way, would you care to join me for a cup of coffee in the library?"

"I don't drink coffee," was all Tess could manage to say. He wasn't married. Danger signals went off in her brain. There went her safe fantasy.

"I think they also have cookies and punch." He rose, waiting.

She wished she could say she didn't drink punch or eat cookies but that would be a bald-faced lie. Sweets were her weakness or at least one of them. "First, I need to sign up for a conference."

After she put her name on the list for an evening meeting with Mrs. Young, she left the classroom. Zachariah was standing in the hallway outside the door, casually leaning against the wall with his arms folded over his chest. His gaze swept down her length in an appreciative survey that produced a tingling sensation in the pit of her stomach.

"How do your sons like Will Rogers Elementary School?" he asked, pushing himself away from the wall.

Tess fell into step beside Zachariah, trusting he knew the way to the library. "Shaun's doing fine. He's met a few friends and has even gone over to several boys' houses. But Wesley, my first grader, is having trouble adjusting."

"How so?" Zachariah placed his hand at her elbow to guide her toward the door into the library.

Tess felt the touch like a brand searing her skin with

his mark. For a few seconds her mind refused to function. He asked her a question. She was sure of it, but for the life of her she couldn't remember what they had been talking about. Oh, my, he was definitely dangerous for her.

"I'm sorry I didn't mean to pry. First grade can be hard to adjust to for any kid let alone one that has just moved here." He steered her toward the refreshment table before releasing his thought-stealing touch.

"Oh, no. That's okay. Wesley has always been shy, slow to make friends. But all he does is go to school, then come home and play in his room by himself. He won't even have anything to do with his older brother. Now, that's out of character. He used to follow Shaun everywhere. I'm worried." Tess took the punch the woman behind the table held out to her and also two big chocolate chip cookies. She would pay for these tomorrow. After work she would have to run an extra mile for each one.

"Time will probably take care of the problem. A lot is happening to Wesley with a new town and school." Zachariah sat at a table across from Tess.

Her stomach knotted with a finely honed tension, and she knew that even if they sat across the room she would feel his presence. "I hope you're right," she finally murmured, realizing she had to say something.

"Of course I am. I'm always right," he said with a laugh.

"How can I argue with a man who saved me a bunch of money today?"

"A wise lady. I like that." He took a sip of his coffee. "When do you start work?"

"Tomorrow eight sharp. I think part of the reason they hired me was because I could start right away. They were desperate. They won't regret it, though."

"Carson International is a good organization."

"There's a lot of opportunities for advancement." She shook her head frowning. "I can't believe I said that. I'd rather be home with the children than craving my niche in the business world." Shrugging, she added, "Oh, well, you have to do what you have to do."

"Children are expensive."

"You have an eighteen-month-old. Where does she stay when you work?"

"My next door neighbor keeps several children. Emily adores her. What are you going to do about Katie?"

"My grandmother will watch her. Granny Kime loves kids. I haven't seen her this excited in a long time." Tess didn't add that she had been the deciding factor in moving to Cimarron City. As much as she wanted to go it alone, she also knew when she needed help at least until she got herself established.

"And your car?"

"Ah, the policeman in you can't rest. I will get it fixed as soon as I get my first paycheck. Two weeks." Tess bit into the cookie, savoring the chunks of chocolate that melted in her mouth.

"I'm not sure fixing something that is dying is good enough. Might be a waste of your hard-earned money."

"I don't have a choice. Buying even a used car is out of the question for the time being. At least this one is paid for."

"But will it do the job?" he asked, finishing his coffee.

"My luck has got to change."

Chapter Two

So much for her luck changing, Tess thought as she tried to crank her engine one more time. Dead. Nothing. *Nada.*

She watched the cars go around her at the stoplight where hers had died and wished she was any place but here. A few people honked, and she sank deeper into the cushion of her seat, trying to decide what to do about her car stuck in the middle of rush hour traffic, what there was in a town of forty thousand.

Finally after the fifth person had laid on his horn to demonstrate his impatience, Tess got out of her car and carefully made her way to the front. She lifted the hood and stared at the lifeless piece of junk under it. She might as well be staring at the Rosette Stone; she wouldn't be able to figure out what was wrong. Brad had always taken care of the car.

She would leave the hood up and call someone to come pick her up. But who? She didn't know anyone in Cimarron City except Granny Kime and she didn't drive anymore.

Maybe one of her grandmother's friends? Frustration mixed with panic began to rise in Tess. She had to get to work on time. This was her first day and being at Carson International at eight was her top priority. After that she would figure out what to do with her car.

After securing the hood up, she glanced around to see if there was a public phone anywhere nearby. She didn't notice the police car pulling up until she heard the door slam close and saw Zachariah Smith striding toward her. Her heart responded with a traitorous beat that had everything to do with the evening before. When he removed his sunglasses and pocketed them, her breath shortened. When he smiled at her, a silver gleam in his eyes, her stomach twisted with electrical tingles.

"So it finally died," he said, peering down at the engine.

"Unless you can perform magic, I'm afraid so."

He went around to the front door and slid into the driver's seat. He tried to start the car but nothing happened. When he poked his head under the hood, probing with his hands for answers, he said, "Not here. I don't have the tools, but I think I can get it running with some work."

"You can?"

"For starters you'll need a new battery and spark plugs. I suspect there will be other things after I get inside and have a close look."

"You're a mechanic, too?"

"Only a hobby. I tinker with my car from time to time."

"And you will mine?"

Zachariah straightened, facing her. "Yes."

"How much?" She thought of her zero bank account balance.

"Dinner with me."

"I hope you like Big Macs. About all I can afford is McDonald's."

"It's my treat."

"Let me get this straight. You will fix my car and take me to dinner, too?"

"Yes."

"I won't take charity," Tess said, determined that he realize she had to stand on her own two feet. Her dependency on a man, which had led her to this point in her life, was over.

"And I'm not giving it. I'll buy the parts and you'll pay me back when you get the money."

"But why are you doing this for me? We barely know each other."

"That's just the point. I want us to get to know each other."

"Oh," she murmured, hearing the danger signals blaring in her mind while her body felt flushed with warmth. She stared down at the dead engine, wishing she had taken an auto mechanics class in school. She didn't want to owe anyone, especially a man who was interested.

"What do you want to do, Tess?"

Run as fast as she could, she thought, looking back up into his face. Before it was too late and she was lost. "This piece of junk is yours. Do with it what you can." As much as she wished she didn't have to, she had to accept his help. This job was too important to her independence, not to mention her ability to feed and clothe her children.

"I'll take you to Carson's and then contact a friend who can tow your car to my house." He started walking toward his vehicle.

Transfixed, Tess felt overwhelmed as though he had breezed into her life and taken over. When he turned at his door, looked at her, one brow arched, and said, "You don't have to go down with the ship. It'll be okay here for an hour or so until I can take care of it," a suffocating panic threatened to cut off her next breath. She needed his help, she reminded herself. She wasn't turning her life over to this man—just her car. Inhaling deep, calming gulps of air, she began to move toward him.

"I insist on taking you out to dinner after I get paid. *My* treat," Tess said as she slipped into the passenger seat.

His gaze snared hers, and she felt probed as he had done the engine a few minutes before—thoroughly and intensely. "Fine. I won't turn down a free meal. I can even eat a Big Mac. It's an occupational duty as a parent."

The tightness about her chest eased. She was in control again. "I think by then I'll be able to swing something where you have to wait for the food to be prepared and someone takes your order while you're sitting down."

"Our McDonald's has a drive through," he quipped and started his engine. "And we could always place a special order."

Tess laughed and completely relaxed while Zachariah maneuvered around her piece of junk and headed for Carson's. "You know I've never ridden in a police car before."

"It's always comforting to know you're not on the ten most wanted list."

"It's so hard to break into the top ten."

His chuckle was low, warm. "I'll be off this afternoon and will take a look at your car. I might be able to fix it today."

"If not, I'd better see if someone at work can come by and pick me up tomorrow morning."

"Will you need a ride home?"

"No," she said quickly, not wanting to be obliged to him anymore than she already was. "You've extended the welcoming mat beyond the call of duty."

He slanted a look toward her. "It's okay to accept help, Tess."

Thankfully they pulled up in front of Carson's and she didn't have to respond to his comment. Instead while he was still inching forward toward the main doors, she jumped out of the car, murmured her thanks, and rushed into the building. Inside she slowed to a sedate pace and headed for the elevator. But she felt his gaze on her, and when she turned from punching her floor number, she saw him through the bank of windows, watching her, a perplexed expression on his face.

Chicken, she thought as the doors swished closed. But in high school she hadn't gone out with a lot of boys and had met Brad her senior year. Her experience with men was very limited and the dating scene almost nonexistent in her life. Suddenly she realized she was twenty-nine years old and starting all over. That realization frightened her more than the day Brad had left her.

"Bruce, come back here," Tess shouted, running around the side of the house, the Great Dane lengthening the distance between them with each leap he took. "Just wait until I get my hands on you."

Bruce raced across the front yard straight toward Zachariah who was getting out of her car. He stopped and looked at the huge dog barreling down on him then at her. Before he had a chance to move, Bruce lunged at the man, plopping his big paws on Zachariah's shoulders and licking him all over his face.

"Stop, Bruce, this instant." Tess rushed forward, praying her Great Dane didn't take Zachariah down with him as he had done the postman.

When her foot hit the slippery slide and went out from under her, the next thing she felt was the hard impact of the ground as her bottom smacked into the yellow, wet plastic and the breath swooshed from her lungs. For a few seconds she sucked in no air and the world spun before her eyes. Then all of a sudden she felt a tongue laved her face, and she was staring into two brown eyes inches from hers while her dog knocked her backward. She locked her arms around Bruce's neck and tried to hold him still.

"Get the leash from my pocket and put it on him. I don't dare let go," Tess said to Zachariah who cautiously approached dog and mistress, both sprawled on the lawn.

When Zachariah's hand slipped into the front pocket of her jeans to pull the leash free, her body reacted as though he had caressed her. Her heart rate that had been slowing after her mad dash accelerated. His male scent overpowered the wet odor of her dog. The touch of his fingers that brushed across her arm as he tried to hook the leather strap onto the collar chased away any chill she felt at the water soaking her back now as well as her front.

"Got him," Zachariah announced triumphantly and stepped away with the leash in his hand.

Tess released her hold on Bruce and scooted back, not sure she should try and attempt to stand just yet. Her legs felt weak like pieces of cooked spaghetti.

She looked up at Zachariah, who was keeping a wary eye on her dog, and saw that his shirt was wet where Bruce had put his paws. Then her gaze traveled lower, taking in the black T-shirt that was stretched over a chest full of muscles, the trim, flat stomach that denoted a man who did a lot of sit ups, the white runner shorts that emphasized the length and strength of his legs. Zachariah Smith was in great shape, she thought and wondered what that body would feel like meshed against hers. For a brief moment she could picture them in her mind and heat suffused her. Gasping, she dropped her gaze to her dog where hopefully her thoughts could conjured up something safe to think about. This man certainly wasn't.

"What do I do with him now that I have him?" Zachariah asked, amusement thick in his voice as if he could read her mind.

Before Tess could answer, Bruce shook himself, sending a shower of water everywhere, peppering Zachariah down his front. Her gaze caught his and she laughed. "What would you like to do with him?"

"The dog catcher is a good friend of mine. I'm sure he wouldn't mind working overtime to relieve the town of this menace."

The laughter in his eyes negated the words, but Tess realized she needed to take control of Bruce before there really was a need for a dog catcher. She slowly rose, aware of the pain in her bottom, of the fact that her wet T-shirt was plastered to her, revealing her figure more than she thought was proper. "You can't possibly mean Bruce. He loves to greet people."

"By bathing them?"

"He got away from me when I was giving him a bath in the wading pool. I should have waited for Shaun to help me. I'm beginning to think Bruce was giving me one, not the other way around."

"I don't mean the shower. I mean the tongue washing."

"Oh, that. I'm afraid so. He's never met a person he didn't like. He's affectionate. The postman got it worse than you. Bruce had the man pinned to the ground, licking his face. When we left New Orleans, the man actually came over and helped me pack." She realized she was chattering again and finished with, "Once you get to know Bruce, though, he's no problem."

"No problem?" Zachariah cocked one brow. "I can't wait to see that."

The implications of his statement jolted her. Underneath his words there was a hint of a future between them. Her nerves quivered with that thought. "Here let me tie him up out back so he can dry before going inside. I can't wait until I can afford to fence in Granny Kime's backyard. I hate having to tie him up."

"You let him inside. What's the insurance company have to say about that?"

"The problem would be if we didn't let him inside. He

would cause such a racket the neighbors would all pitch in to help us move." She grinned. "We seem to have that kind of effect on people."

Tess took the leash and tried to pull Bruce along behind her, muttering dire threats if the beast didn't follow her since she knew it would be impossible for her to drag one hundred fifty pounds of Great Dane across the grass. Clearly the dog didn't want to leave his new friend, but something in the tone of her voice must have alerted him to his precarious situation. Bruce took one last look at Zachariah, then bounded after Tess.

While she hooked the dog to the rope used to keep him in the backyard, she heard the jingle of the ice cream truck as it came down the street. After the past week she thought she had convinced the young man not to come down Oakcrest.

Tess ran toward the front of the house, her feet pounded against the ground like her heart was against her breast. She prayed her daughter was occupied and didn't hear the truck. As Tess rounded the corner, she saw Katie streak across the lawn into the street and lay down on the pavement in the path of the oncoming vehicle. As quickly as Katie moved, Zachariah moved faster once he saw her intention. He scooped her up in his arms as the truck came to a screeching halt a few feet away from them.

The alarm in Zachariah's expression when he swung around to face Tess contrasted with the laughter bubbling up from her daughter's throat. Katie wound her arms around his neck and said, "Whee. I like dat. Twirl me around some more."

Tess stopped, plunged her fingers through her curls, and held her head as she shook it. She counted to ten, trying to calm herself before she spoke to her daughter; Tess had to go straight for one hundred. As the young man behind the wheel staggered out of the truck, terror on his face, she said, "Katie, go to your room." Tess was amazed her voice sounded so level while inside she quaked.

"But I want an ice cream cone."

"You won't get ice cream for the next month, possibly your entire life. Go." Tess pointed toward the house as Zachariah placed Katie on the ground.

Katie looked up at Tess, stuck her thumb in her mouth, and stomped off toward the front steps. "I never get ice cream. It's not fair."

Tess waited until her daughter was safely inside the house, then approached the young man who was shaking like a flag in a stiff breeze. "Didn't Al tell you not to come down this street?"

"No, ma'am."

"My daughter has an unorthodox way of trying to get ice cream. She loves chocolate and once Al didn't stop so the next time she made sure he did by lying in the street in front of the truck. I'm sorry about this. Al and I had this understanding."

"He was sick. I was just filling in for the day." The young man backed away from Tess as if she had a contagious disease he would get any second. He hopped into the truck and tore out of there with tires screeching.

"I don't think he'll be filling in for Al again," Tess said as she watched the poor driver take the corner way too fast and dangerously. "Shouldn't you go after him or something?"

"The boy's long gone by now. Besides, with the scare he just had, I doubt he would hear a word I said."

"Yeah, I guess you're right. His face was as white as the vanilla ice cream he sells."

"Tess Morgan, I must admit you have an interesting family and I've only met one of your children."

"I can't say that I ever have a dull day. I'm glad I don't care about a routine schedule."

"Go with the flow?"

"And then some." Tess pointed toward her car. "You got it fixed."

"For the time being, but there are no guarantees."

"How much?" She tensed, expecting to hear the national debt quoted.

"Two hundred."

"Is that all?" Relief trembled through her.

He handed her the bill for the parts. "Yes, Mack and I have an arrangement. You can pay him off in installments over the next several months."

She noticed the name of the store was Mack's Auto Park. "Thank you. Come on in and have something to drink."

"Is it safe? Where's Bruce?"

"Tied securely out back." Tess smiled at the light tone in Zachariah's voice. She suspected he had taken care of a lot worse threats than a Great Dane named Bruce.

"Well, in that case, I'd like something to drink."

Tess began walking toward the house. "I have lemonade and iced tea. Which will it be?"

Giggles erupted right before first one balloon then another sputtered in the grass next to Zachariah's feet, drenching his tennis shoes and socks. "A towel first then a glass of iced tea," he replied without missing a beat as though he had unexpected things thrown at him every day.

Tess stopped, blew out a breath of air, and scanned the limbs of the oak. "Shaun Franklin Morgan, you get down here right this minute and bring your friend." As the two boys clamored down the tree, she muttered to Zachariah, "My children really do know how to behave—most of the time."

When Shaun and Freddie stood in front of her, she placed her hands on her hips and a stern expression on her face. "What's the meaning of this." She gestured at the remnants of the red balloons in the grass."

"It was on accident. I swear, Mom."

"Oh, I see. Water just appeared in the balloon and it just slipped from your fingers not one time but twice."

"I was handing both of them to Freddie to hold. We're stockpiling for our war."

"What war?"

"The Roberts brothers down the street."

"You're fighting?"

"No, playing, Mom. We were lying in wait for them to come over. We're going to ambush them." Shaun's tone conveyed that mothers didn't know anything about the fine art of warfare.

"Well, you're going to have to ambush them somewhere else. We have a guest. Shaun, I would like you to meet Officer Smith. And this is my son's cohort, Freddie, who lives down the street." Tess gestured toward the boy next to her son.

Shaun's eyes grew round. "A policeman?"

Zachariah nodded, holding out his hand to shake with the boys'.

"Where's your gun?" Shaun asked, moving closer to Zachariah.

"I'm not on duty. It's at home."

"Can I see it sometime?"

Zachariah glanced at Tess, a question in his gray eyes.

She put her hand on her son's shoulder and turned him toward her. "We'll see about that some other time, Shaun. You boys clean this mess up. And don't use the oak tree as your base. People walk by here. We're new in town. We have to at least make a good first impression."

"Nice to meet you, Shaun, Freddie," Zachariah said, the corners of his mouth twitching in silent laughter.

Tess resumed walking toward the house, praying Wesley didn't jump out from behind the bushes in front of the porch. When Zachariah and she safely made it up the steps and to the door, she breathed easier. After they were inside, she indicated a seat in the living room while she went into the kitchen to get the iced teas and towels for both of them.

When she brought the drinks into the room, Tess found Katie sitting on the couch next to Zachariah, staring at him while she sucked her thumb. He had said something to her, but she hadn't responded.

Tess placed the glasses on coasters on the coffee table, then handed Zachariah one of the towels. "I don't remember telling you to come out of your room, young lady."

Katie removed her thumb from her mouth, her gaze still glue on Zachariah. "What's your name? Why are you here? Do you have any children? Do you live near here?"

"Excuse me," Tess said and took her daughter's hand. "I'll be right back." She marched Katie down the hall and opened the door to her daughter's bedroom. "You will not come out until I say so. Understand?"

"But, Mommie, I'm hungry. I won't do dat anymore. I promise." Katie looked up at her with her big brown eyes and a sad expression on her face.

Tess could swear her daughter practiced "that look" in front of the mirror. "We'll talk later." Tess guided Katie inside her room, then shut the door, hoping after the kind of day she'd had that her patience would last past dinner and the discussion she would have with her youngest.

"Sorry about that," Tess said, sitting down across from Zachariah after toweling herself as dry as possible. "I doubt the mother on the *Brady Bunch* ever had this kind of problem."

"My role model is Robert Anderson from *Father Knows Best*. How does a father live up to that?" He took a long sip of his iced tea. "All problems solved within thirty minutes."

"Being a parent is the hardest job around and you don't have to have any qualifications to apply."

"If it's any comfort, I felt right at home out in that front yard. I know my daughter, Emily, is only eighteen months, but she's so curious the only way I can baby proof the house is to remove everything."

Tess laughed. "I once found Katie up on the top shelf of the bookcase because she wanted to look at the figurine I had put up there. I soon discovered there was no 'out of reach' zone in my house with her. She could climb like a monkey."

"And I'd always heard boys were the active ones. I thought Emily would be a cinch compared to Lance. I'm finding out I thought wrong."

"We're having spaghetti tonight. You're welcome to stay for dinner. I can't tell you how much I appreciate you getting my car to run again."

"Not tonight. Lance has soccer practice," Zachariah looked at his watch, "in thirty minutes. I'm the coach. But I'll take a rain check on that invitation. I sure get tired of cooking, especially when all my children eat are macaroni and cheese, peanut butter and jelly sandwiches, and pizza, the big three at the Smith household."

"Wait till you get to add things like hamburgers and french fries and bologna sandwiches. You'll think you died and gone to heaven."

"Oh, something to look forward to. I can hardly wait."

She picked up her iced tea and held it cradled in her lap. "Well, then I promise when you come for dinner I'll have something to dazzle your taste buds for us grown-ups."

"Now that really is something to look forward to."

The smile he gave her melted her insides. The look in his eyes warmed her outside, two patches of red staining her cheeks. The promise of things to come hung in the air between them. Tess gripped her glass tighter and downed half her ice cold drink, her eyes never leaving his.

"I think I'd better get going or the coach will be late for practice. I would hate to have to run laps."

"Wesley was on a team last fall. He showed promise. I wish he would play again."

"Have him come to practice one day. We haven't been working out very long. The season just got under way. We could always use another player." Zachariah rose and started toward the door.

"He tells me he doesn't want to play. He doesn't want to do anything but build with his Legos in his room by himself," Tess said, following Zachariah to show him out.

He turned suddenly at the door, only inches from her. "I have a great idea. Why don't I take you and your children on a fishing expedition and picnic this Saturday? It'll give Lance and Wesley a chance to get to know each other outside of the classroom."

She hesitated. One part of her wanted to grab at the chance to be with this man, to have Wesley get to know Lance, but the other part warned her of the danger of getting involved with the Smith family and especially one Zachariah Smith. She never did anything halfway. She tended to throw herself wholeheartedly into a project which would only cause her pain later because she would not turn her life over to another person ever again and Officer Smith was a take charge kind-of guy.

"There's a neat fishing hole I discovered at Beaver Lake. I'm willing to share the secret with your family."

Share. Something Brad had never done, Tess thought. She had to do it for Wesley, she told herself. "Okay. What time?"

"Nine. I'll pick you all up. I don't know if your car would make it and mine seats eight."

"Do you want a ride home? You don't have much time before practice."

"Naw. I like to run. It's only four blocks. It keeps me in shape," he said as he opened the screen door and jogged down the steps, waving good-bye.

Again Tess thought of that body that was in better shape

than most and she felt the constriction in her chest, the beat of her heart increase. And she would be near that magnificent bod for a whole day. "Thank goodness for five children. The best chaperons in the world," she muttered, watching him disappear down the street.

Zachariah knew she was watching him as he jogged away. He felt her eyes on him as though they physically were touching him. He missed a step, throwing himself off rhythm. She had a way of doing that, he acknowledged to himself. Saturday should be a very interesting day. Sort of like running through a minefield, he decided as he turned the corner to his street, remembering feeling that way when he had first arrived at her place.

He loped up to his neighbor's house to get Emily. Nora opened the door and called out to his daughter who raced toward him.

"Da Dee." Emily threw her arms around his legs and held on. "Pick up."

He scooped his daughter up and whirled her around and around. Latching onto his neck, she giggled and planted a big kiss on his cheek.

When he stopped, she said, "'Gain, Da Dee."

"Can't, sugar. Lance has soccer practice. He's already at the field. We need to get going ourselves." He swung her up on his shoulders, said good-bye to Nora, and headed for their place.

When he stepped inside, he put his daughter down and looked around. He missed having a woman about. He missed sharing his day with someone other than a person under four feet. Most of all he missed the companionship. Instantly he pictured Tess moving about his house, giving his home her personal touches, being a part of his life. He liked that picture, but he knew a wary lady when he saw one. Tess Morgan was running scared and he intended to catch her.

Chapter Three

"Are we there yet?" Katie asked for the twentieth time in the past ten minutes.

"Almost. We've pulled off the main highway," Tess said as she twisted around.

"Da Dee, pick up." Strapped into her child safety seat, Emily held her arms up, wiggling her fingers.

"Not yet, sugar. Two minutes to Beaver Lake." Zachariah slanted a glance toward Tess and grinned.

She returned his smile. "You know I realize it's only been thirty minutes since we left my house, but it feels like two hours. Traveling with kids could have been a successful torture back in the days of the Spanish Inquisition."

"When I moved here from Chicago, I paid Lance a dollar an hour to keep quiet about how much longer we had to go. I believe it saved my sanity. And of course, thankfully Emily couldn't talk yet."

"How long have you been in Cimarron City? I thought you were a native."

"Sixteen months," Zachariah answered as he pulled under a large cottonwood tree and parked.

Before Tess could say a word, two doors flew open and three children leaped from the car and raced for the water. While Emily kept asking her father to pick her up, Tess fumbled with her door handle, trying to get out. Katie was right behind Shaun and Lance. Panic fueled Tess's determination as she wrenched open the door and bounded from the car.

"Katie! Stop this minute!" With her heart in her throat, Tess watched as her daughter came to a halt and whirled about. Relieved that Katie for once had listened to her, Tess hurried toward her, not sure how long her daughter would stay put.

"Mommie, I want to go wif Shaun." Katie bounced from one foot to the other as though she couldn't contain her energy.

"Not until you put on your life preserver."

"Shaun and Wesley don't have to wear one." Katie's lower lip puckered out, her tiny fists resting on her hips.

"They know how to swim. You don't." Tess clasped her daughter's hand and started back toward the car, practically dragging a stubborn four-year-old who had literally dug in her heels. "We can always go home."

Reluctantly Katie followed, her thumb in her mouth. "It's not fair."

"If I had a dollar for every time I heard those words, I'd be rich," Tess muttered, and retrieved the life preserver from the back of the van. After securing the vest on Katie, Tess quickly grabbed her daughter before she raced off and added, "You have to stay by the boys and you can't go into the water. Okay?"

Katie nodded, then shot off after the boys who were at the edge of the lake skipping rocks. Her daughter immediately picked up a pebble that was too big and tried to mimic her older brother. The uncooperative stone plopped into the water with a splash not two feet from shore.

"Tess, Wesley's still in the car," Zachariah said as he held a squirming Emily.

Tess sighed, pushed her curls off her forehead, and headed for the front of the van. She climbed into the third seat where Wesley sat and stared out the window. With Emily tucked under one arm, giggling, Zachariah took the last piece of fishing equipment out of the back and closed the doors, leaving silence to reign in the van.

"Wesley, aren't you going to join Shaun and Lance?"

"Don't wanna," he mumbled, his forehead pressed to the glass.

"Zachariah is gonna show Shaun how to fish. You don't want to learn, too?"

Wesley shook his head.

Tess laid a hand on his shoulder, a lump in her throat. He hadn't said much when she had announced the plans for the day. He had just disappeared into his room and continued to build some kind of contraption with his Legos. She kneaded his taut muscles and searched for the magic words to bring her son back to her and the family.

"Honey, you can't sit in the van all day. It's too hot."

He shrugged her hand off his shoulder and turned completely away from her. "I don't feel like fishing."

"But Lance is sharing one of his fishing poles with you."

"I don't care."

Tears burned in her eyes as she watched her son draw further within himself. Ever since Brad had left, Wesley had grown more withdrawn with each day and she wasn't sure what to do about it.

After a few minutes of uncomfortable silence, Tess said, "If you change your mind, you know where we are. I hope you'll join us soon." She scooted from the van and left the sliding door open so fresh air could circulate. That was all she could do for her son, all he would allow her to do.

Tears still pricked her eyes as she walked over to Zachariah, Emily and Granny Kime. They were setting up the chairs and a blanket under the shade of an oak tree. Swallowing hard several times, Tess forced a smile to her lips. "What can I do?"

Zachariah placed Emily on a blanket surrounded by her toys. "We're through here."

"You two run along," Granny Kime said as she pulled her folding chair up close to Emily and picked up a children book to read to the baby. "I'll watch her."

"Thanks," Zachariah said, then grasped Tess's hand. "Come with me."

The comfort of his fingers about hers eased the constriction in her throat. She blinked away her tears and allowed him to lead her away.

"I gather Wesley isn't joining us."

"No, he won't even look at the boys at the lake. He's staring off into the underbrush."

His hand tightened about hers. "Can I help? Do you want me to talk with Wesley?"

Part of her wanted to turn the problem over to Zachariah, but she just couldn't say yes. Wesley was her son, her problem. "I'll talk with him again in an hour. Maybe by then he'll be bored or hungry and want to come out of the van."

"Tess, all you have to do is ask. I'll help in any way I can."

"You've done more than enough. This outing was for Wesley to get know Lance. I appreciate you trying."

"Dad, come on. Let's fish," Lance shouted from the water's edge.

Tess noticed that Shaun had a hold of Katie's hand and she was tugging on his arm, trying to get away. "I think we'd better get the show on the road. You have three excited children waiting."

"Yes, ma'am." He grinned, giving her a salute. "After all we have freezers to fill and only a few hours to do it in."

As Zachariah strode toward the children, Tess looked back at the van, her heart feeling heavy. Wesley still had his body plastered against the other side away from the action, one of his cheeks pressed against the glass as he stared at his lap. On the drive to the lake Lance had done his best to include Wesley in the conversation, but her son had responded only with one word answers. He had never been as outgoing as Shaun. Wesley eased into friendships with other children, standing back and casing things out before he stepped in. But lately he wouldn't even stay around to watch. Tess flexed her fingers open, then balled them at her sides.

"If I ever get my hands on Brad, I'll gladly wring his neck," she muttered and made her way toward the lake.

"Mom, look at this worm. I put it on the hook." Shaun swung the pole with the dangling bait toward her.

Wrinkling her nose at the squirming worm coming dangerously close, Tess stepped back to avoid it and lost her footing in the gravel. Down she went, slamming her bottom against the hard pebbles by the shore at the same time the disgusting bait ended up in her lap. Surprised, she screamed while the worm wiggled on her shirt. She could hear the children's giggles as Zachariah mercifully retrieved the bait sticking to her clothing. Embarrassment scorched her cheeks red, her gaze remaining glued to the ground at her feet.

Zachariah reached out to give her a hand up. "Is that your favorite way of looking at the world? From the ground up?"

She glanced at his offer of help then up into his face. He was barely containing his laughter, the sparkle in his gray eyes reminding her of polished silver that caught the rays of the sun. Placing her hand in his, she forgot everyone and everything around her for a few seconds. This man was way too appealing for her peace of mind.

His smile. Those eyes. That body! Whoa, get a grip on yourself, Tess Morgan.

With a yank she sprang to her feet, rubbing her sore bottom. "At least Bruce isn't here to slobber all over me."

"You have to count your blessings anyway you can and not bringing that monster was one of them," Zachariah said with a deep chuckle as though he were visualizing the scene in her front yard when she had skidded on the slippery slide and landed in the same predicament. "Thank goodness we were able to prevail over the kids' demands to bring Bruce with us."

"Prevail? Weren't you the one who tried to get him into the van?"

"And couldn't. That was my strategy. I proved there was no earthly way to bring Bruce and they all quit whining."

"Only after your promise to take them to get ice cream on the way home from the lake."

"Bribery has its place in the scheme of things." He held a pole out for her as well as a worm. "Are you going to fish? I'll share mine."

"I don't think so," she answered, pronouncing each word slowly as she took a careful step backward. "I'll just watch."

"I'll bait your hook." The amused sparkle in his eyes brightened.

"I don't think I have any patience for fishing. Besides, didn't you tell the boys what they catch they get to clean?" She could remember in the car the enthusiastic yells to that declaration.

"I could use any fish you catch to demonstrate with. They'll never know you're squeamish."

"Squeamish! Me! I've changed more diapers than most."

"That's different, Tess."

"How so?"

"You didn't have a choice."

"Okay, I'll admit that the idea of gutting a fish isn't high on my to do list. I'll watch."

She marched back to the oak tree. With a glance toward the van, she noticed Wesley was now staring out the window at them, not into the underbrush or at his lap. A good sign, she decided, her step lightening.

Emily had fallen asleep on the blanket clutching a stuffed bear. Granny Kime had her knitting needles out and was busy working on a sweater for Katie. Tess took a folding chair and carried it back to the water where she sat gingerly, her bottom still sore from her encounter with the ground. She would give Wesley another hour then see if she could persuade him to join them.

During the hour wait Zachariah caught one fish, Katie two, Lance four and Shaun none. Tess watched Zachariah patiently help Katie bait her hook and cast, untangling her line several times. Tess watched him instruct Shaun in the finer points of fishing. She watched him move between the children with a supple fluidity that was no doubt an asset on his job. He was wonderful with the kids. A terrific dad, she thought, but caught herself before she took the fantasy any further.

"I haven't caught any fish," Shaun checked for the hundredth time if he still had a worm on the end of his line.

"Maybe you should cast out farther where the water is deeper," Zachariah said, coming up behind the boy.

Shaun stepped to the edge of the huge boulder he was standing on and rocked back and forth on the balls of his feet, working himself up to cast his line. Again then again he flicked his rod as though he were going to let go but didn't. Then when he finally did, he catapulted himself into the lake before Zachariah could catch him. The rod went sailing across the water as Shaun bobbed to the surface, laughing.

While Lance and Katie giggled, Zachariah shielded his eyes and looked out where the rod landed. "I think that's about right. Now all you'll have to do is learn to hold on."

Shaun waded out of the lake and turned to see where his pole was floating. "I'll get it."

"No, I will," Zachariah said and began to take off his shirt, socks and shoes.

Tess had a front row seat to his "striptease". Her pulse leaped to an alarming rate while he peeled off each sock. Her breathing became shallow as he stood and slid the cotton shirt up his massive chest and over his head, flinging the piece of clothing to the ground. She waved her hand in front of her face as beads of perspiration broke out on her forehead. It was just too darn hot! Maybe she should be the one to offer to get the pole.

While Zachariah swam out to the fishing rod, Wesley came up to stand next to Tess. Wiping her brow with the back of her hand, she slanted a glance toward her middle child.

"Would you like to try this?" she asked Wesley, holding her breath as she waited for his answer.

He nodded, his gaze never leaving the figure of Zachariah as he slid through the water, grabbed the pole and swam back to shore.

When Zachariah emerged from the water, Tess rose and handed him a towel. "Wesley wants to fish."

Zachariah finished drying his hair, then looked at the boy. "Great!" He gestured for Wesley to come with him while he fixed the child up with a fishing pole and bait.

As Tess settled back into the chair, Shaun untangled his line, walked over to the bucket that held the seven fish caught so far and put his hook into the water. "This might be the safest place for me to fish."

Everyone stopped what they were doing and stared at Shaun, then broke out laughing. Tess listened to Wesley and smiled. For the first time in months she felt hope.

When the doorbell sounded, Tess was closing the door to Katie's bedroom. She had fallen asleep right after dinner, such an unusual occurrence that Tess was still shocked. Quickly before her daughter awakened, Tess hurried toward the front door before the chimes could ring again.

"Hi." Zachariah held up the fish fillets. "These are your half."

Tess took the tray and indicated that he come inside while she put the fish in the refrigerator. When she walked back into the living room, he was no where to be found. She looked in the hall then she heard voices and headed toward Wesley and Shaun's bedroom.

"My big thing was the Star Wars figures. When that first movie came out, I went crazy buying everything there was. It's hard to imagine it's been twenty years. It seems like yesterday that Luke was fighting Darth Vader and flying his X-wing." Zachariah sat on the floor with his long legs crossed Indian style and inspected Wesley's latest warship.

"Do you still have the figures?"

"Yeah, up in the attic. Would you like to see them?"

"Could I?" Wesley's eyes grew round.

"Any time your mom says it's okay."

Wesley glanced up at her. "Can I? Can I, Mom?"

"Sure." Her throat closed about the one word. She hadn't seen this much excitement on her son's face in a year.

Zachariah carefully placed the warship on the floor by Wesley and rose. "Then it's a date. You can come over tomorrow afternoon and look at the whole collection."

When Tess walked him to the door and stepped outside onto the porch, she didn't want the day to end quite yet.

The house was quiet for a change, everyone subdued after the fishing expedition earlier. "Would you like some iced tea?"

"What I would like is for you to sit and talk with me. We hardly had time to get to know each other today." He drew her toward the porch swing and sat, taking her hand and pulling her down next to him.

"I can't imagine why. Just because five children were running around, demanding our time, shouldn't have had any bearing on it. Can't you do two or three things at once?"

The chuckle he emitted was intimate like the night closing in on them. "I've had to learn to. After Laurie died, I had a crash course in being not only a father but a mother. A newborn doesn't wait around until you've passed diapering or feeding."

"But didn't you practice with Lance?" The press of his side against hers made her acutely aware of the dark descending.

"Not nearly enough I soon discovered."

She turned so she could face him, putting her back against the arm of the swing, putting some space between them. "How did you do it?"

"One day at a time. But I realized I had to get out of Chicago. I needed family supports, so I came back to Cimarron City."

"Then you are a native?"

"I was born here. Left when I went to college. Now I've come full circle. My father is still alive, some aunts and uncles and a whole bunch of cousins are running around Cimarron City. Great support." He slid his arm along the back of the swing, his hand close to her. "How about you? What made you decide to come here?"

"My grandmother. Did Lance help you finish filleting the fish?"

"Yes. But you weren't raised here. I would have known

that." His look seared her, leaving a burning path as it roamed over her features. "Definitely I would have known. Is your grandmother from here?"

"No. How big is your collection of Star War figures? Wesley had a friend in New Orleans who had his dad's collection. They used to play for hours."

"Big enough to fill a chest. I was really into it for a few years before I became too old." His forefinger grazed a heated trail down her upper arm. So where did you grow up? New Orleans?"

"No. I used to have a Barbie doll collection that I hope one day Katie will appreciate."

His finger stopped at the pulse beat at her wrist. "Why are you avoiding my questions?"

Tess shivered. "I answered them."

His hand slid back up her arm. "I suppose technically you did."

She looked down at his fingers on her skin and everything inside her began to unravel. "I was born in Tulsa."

"How did you end up in New Orleans?"

"After I married Brad, we moved there because of his job."

"How did your grandmother end up here?"

"Her best friend lives here because of her family. Granny Kime didn't like how big Tulsa was getting so she moved. There wasn't anything keeping her there once I left."

"See now that wasn't so bad." His hand found its way to her shoulder and began to massage.

Suddenly Tess realized there was no space between them, that he had inched closer until she could inhale his distinctive male scent, could see the lightning glitter in his eyes, could feel his presence in every fiber of her body. He overwhelmed her.

"Will you bring Wesley over tomorrow?"

Her thoughts were dissolving as quickly as sugar in hot water. She tried to concentrate on his question, but the feel of his fingers kneading her shoulder obliterated all reasoning. She leaned closer, as though seeking the warmth of his body.

"Will you come tomorrow, Tess?"

His whispered question penetrated her dazed mind, and she nodded.

"Good." He lifted his thumb to outline the curve of her mouth. The rough texture of his skin against hers sent a quiver down her length. "How was your first half-week of work?"

Work? Was he talking about something rational? Tess's bemused mind asked while his hand glided down to the curve of her neck and explored. She inhaled deeply, held it.

"Is everything going okay at Carson's?"

Even though the shadows of night were enclosing about them, Tess could see the intensity in his eyes. She blinked, looking away. "It will be a demanding job, but I think I'm going to love it." Her words came out in a breathless rush as she tried to bring a semblance of order to the chaos his touch was producing in her.

"That's great," he murmured, bending toward her, his mouth an inch away from hers. "It makes it so much easier when you like your job."

His mint scented breath bathed her lips. Tess slid her eyes closed and anticipated the kiss to come with a wholeheartedness she was known for. With the first brush of his mouth across hers, she felt lost. With the second then the third, she melted against him. With the total possession of his lips, she wound her arms about him, drowning in one shattering sensation after another.

He slanted her back on the swing, fitting his hard body to her soft contours, cushioning her against the wood with his arm. His tongue invaded her mouth, sweeping inside to delve, to thrust. His fingers plunged into her hair, holding her locked against him. His heart pounded against hers almost as though they beat as one, the tempo fast.

She felt surrounded and bewitched at the same time. She sank further and further into a black void where she didn't exist, all her senses centered on Zachariah. Tess Morgan was disappearing. That realization brought forth her alarm and she wrenched away.

His harsh breathing filled the silence as she straightened, trying to bring her own breathing under control. "It's getting late," she said, her voice quavering like her body.

He stood, staring down at her. "What time will you be by tomorrow?"

She definitely felt at a disadvantage with him towering over her. She could see nothing of his expression now that it was totally dark, but she could feel his puzzlement, she could hear him settle his labored breathing. "What time is best for you?"

"Any time after eleven."

Such politeness after such passion, Tess thought, control of her emotions slowly returning to her. "Then we'll be there at one." She rose, even though her legs felt weak, to walk him to the stairs. She had to prove to herself that she wasn't going to be engulfed by a man to the point she ceased to be.

He halted at the bottom step and looked back up at her. "I know what it's like to be scared. I face that every day I go out on my job, but it doesn't stop me," he said, then pivoted and left her.

Tess touched the lips he had totally and ruthlessly possessed such a short time before. She could still remember the feel of them against hers. Maybe Granny Kime could take Wesley to Zachariah's house tomorrow because she just wasn't as brave as he was.

Chapter Four

Tess sat holding Emily while Wesley, Lance and Zachariah were at the kitchen table going through his Star Wars collection. Watching her son's expression blossom into joy made Tess glad she had given in to Wesley's demand and come to Zachariah's house instead of Granny Kime. Tess knew it wasn't because her son didn't love his great grandmother, but Tess recognized the insecurity on his face the second he turned it up toward hers and realized she couldn't deny him his simple request to accompany him, even though her common sense told her otherwise.

She felt a tug on her earring and looked down at Emily. Thankfully she hadn't worn her dangling ones, Tess thought as she smiled at the little girl. Her gray eyes, so much like her father's, were filled with such concentration on the glittering gold of the stud.

"Pret-tee," Emily said while her chubby little fingers tried to pull on the earring.

Before the child ripped a hole in her earlobe, Tess grabbed at the nearest diversion she could find, a Star War figure of some grotesque alien, and handed it to Emily. "Look at this."

The eighteen-month-old immediately followed her direction—probably one of the last times she would be so cooperative since the terrible twos loomed ahead—and began to examine the figure, first with her eyes then her mouth. A minute later she lost interested and was back to trying to pry off the earring.

Tess shifted the child in her lap so she could take off her gold studs and put them in her jeans pocket. Out of sight, out of mind was an adage Tess believed in, at least for small children. When it came to herself, it didn't work. All the night before she had tossed and turned, dreaming and thinking about the man across from her. It scared her how quickly he had ingrained himself into her life. This morning over breakfast all Shaun and Katie had talked about was their fishing expedition and when could they go again with Zachariah.

"Mom, look at this one. He's got Chewbacca."

"Han Solo's friend?" Emily squirmed in Tess's arm. She switched the little girl to her other side, hoping the small change of scenery would satisfy the child.

"Yeah, isn't he neat? Mr. Smith even has his weapon."

Tess's gaze fastened onto Zachariah's. "Why do boys love weapons? I wouldn't allow toy guns in the house. Guess what both Shaun and Wesley did."

"Made their own," Zachariah said, his eyes warming to a molten silver.

"Or used their fingers." Tess knew she should look away from the male approval in his gaze. In fact, she should run now, but for the life of her she couldn't move a muscle. Everything was eclipsed by him, the world about them fading from perception. All she could focus on was the sensuous lift of his mouth, the sexy gleam in his look, the confidant set of his features. Her thoughts scattered in a hundred different directions as though they were seeds carried by the wind.

"It's the power thing," Zachariah said, a playfully wicked sparkle in his eyes now.

"Is that the reason when they grow up they still love weapons?"

"Who said anything about growing up." Laughter laced Zachariah's voice as the lines at the corners of his eyes deepened.

"Mom, I don't use my fingers anymore." Wesley looked from his mother to Zachariah then back to her.

"Oh, yeah." Tess tore her gaze away from Zachariah's. For a few seconds she had forgotten that there were three children in the room which was quite a feat since Emily was tugging on her T-shirt and Tess hadn't even noticed. Could women have a bad case of hormonal overload? "I forgot you like to use your Legos now."

"Legos!" Lance exclaimed, jumping to his feet. "You should see my sets. C'mon, Wesley, I'll show them to you."

Wesley glanced uncertainly at Lance then at Tess. Her son chewed on his bottom lip, poised on the edge of his seat as though hovering between two attractive choices. "Go on, Wesley. I'll be in here with Mr. Smith and Emily."

Wesley leaped up and raced after Lance. Tess shook her head as her gaze followed the boys' progress from the room. "There is no halfway with kids. It's either standstill or run." She yanked on her shirt, trying to dislodge Emily's tight hold on it before Tess was exposed to Zachariah. She couldn't believe the cotton material could be stretched that far.

He watched the tug-of-war between Emily and Tess, his eyes taking on a dreamy quality. "Standstill? You have that at your house?"

She had to look down to free herself from the little girl's clutches. When she lifted her head, she found Zachariah still staring at her, a sexual appeal in his gaze, and the blush that came so easily to her flamed her cheeks. "When they're sleeping," she murmured, not even sure where her reply had come from.

"Ah, the best time of the day. And speaking of sleeping. It's time for Emily's nap."

Breaking their visual link, he took his daughter from Tess, cradling his child in the crook of his arm with such tenderness that emotions swelled inside Tess. Emily smiled up at her father, then laid her head on his shoulder, her eyes already drooping closed. Zachariah brushed a wisp of his daughter's hair back from her forehead and bent his head to kiss her where the strand had lain.

How many times had she wished that Brad would have cared enough to hold his children like that? Tess wondered as the thickness in her throat grew. Now she realized they had never really been a family, doing things together and sharing the way families did. They had never gone on a fishing expedition like the day before.

"All you have to do is mention the word nap and she's nodding off. I'm impressed," Tess said, again uncomfortably aware of the pull this man had on her, of the fact that with him her children had more a sense of what family was than when their father had been around.

"Don't be. It's an hour passed her nap time and I could see she was working herself up with her restlessness."

"I am impressed. You know your daughter well."

"It's called survival. You either learn real fast to read the subtle and not so subtle signs or you deal with the tantrum that follows. It didn't take many tantrums for me to figure out what to do most of the time."

"Yeah, but just about the time you think you have it down pat they start another stage in their life and you have to start all over."

"And this next stage isn't one I'm looking forward to. I'll be right back," Zachariah said over his shoulder as he started out of the kitchen.

"Don't hurry on my account." Tess suddenly felt the potential intimacy of her situation. Even though a kitchen wasn't a particularly romantic room, she didn't think it much mattered where they were alone together or for that matter where they weren't alone together. He dominated and occupied a space with his commanding presence that she was having a hard time fighting by herself or with children surrounding her.

Tess drew in a deep, stabilizing breath. The heat in the room must have soared ten degrees in the past hour. She shot to her feet and began to prowl, restless as though she needed to shed a layer of skin. He was just a man, she told herself as she walked from one end of the kitchen to the other. Then she remembered that man holding his baby daughter in his arms and her heart thudded. She remembered his laughter which came so easily to him and she remembered his eyes that could almost physically possess her. But most of all she remembered his kiss the evening before that had produced a sleepless night of fantasizing what it would be like to have his body pressed to her, to have his mouth making love to her.

Tess fanned herself. Was his air conditioner working properly? A bead of perspiration broke out on her forehead. Maybe she should say something to him about having his air conditioner fixed.

"She's down for the count, I think," Zachariah said as he came back into the room.

"I wish Katie still took naps." Tess latched onto the safe subject and kept her distance.

"That's one thing I'm thankful for. Emily still takes two naps a day and they're usually pretty long ones." He stood across the room from Tess, folding his arms over his chest, leaning casually back against the doorjamb. "I also checked on the boys. Lance is showing Wesley all his different Lego sets. Wesley isn't saying much, but he's acting interested."

Tess ran her hand back and forth along the counter top. "I hope your son can work miracles with Wesley like you did with my car."

"I gather then that it's still running."

"Yes and I even got my safety sticker thanks to you fixing my muffler."

"Among other things." He shoved himself away from the doorjamb and strode further into the room.

Tess gripped the counter top as Zachariah stopped only a foot away from her. "Boy, I'm glad you checked the lights. I didn't even know that the left taillight wasn't working. Who goes around the back of his car and checks his brake lights? Now the muffler I couldn't miss. It loudly proclaimed something was wrong, but the—"

He lifted his hand and placed a finger over her mouth to still her nervous prattle. "When I do a job, I'm always thorough."

Her heartbeat raced. Her mouth went dry. She wet her lips with her tongue and knew instantly the mistake she had made. Zachariah's gaze flared with a searing heat as it locked onto her moistened mouth. His hands slid into her short curls and held her still while he lowered his head toward hers.

"When I go after something, I don't stop until I get it," he whispered against her mouth, his breath blending with hers. "I thought we would never be alone."

Then he claimed her lips in a kiss. The world of darkness swirled behind her closed eyelids as Tess clutched his shoulders to steady herself. His tongue invaded the hot moistness of her mouth much as the man was invading her life—boldly, sweepingly.

Their bodies melded as completely as their breaths, their mouths, their tongues. The compelling danger in his embrace slowly seeped into her dazed mind. The Tess she didn't recognize didn't want to listen to reason. She wanted to cling to the hard planes of his body. She wanted to feel the warmth so long denied. She wanted to experience the feminine pleasure of being desired by a virile man. She wanted to live the fantasy of her dream the night before.

But a painful year of hardships stamped those wants down, and Tess brought her hands up between their meshed bodies and shoved away from him. She needed no other reason than what just happened between them to reinforce her determination to go it alone. Zachariah Smith swamped her, robbing her of her own thoughts and will. Above all else she never wanted again to depend on another so much that his rejection rocked her to her core, shaking the very foundation of herself.

"I think it's time for us to go home," she said, backing away from him until she felt the wall behind her.

"Running won't solve anything."

"Running? We're walking home."

His gaze sharpened on her. "I think we both know you're afraid to explore what's happening between us."

"There's nothing to explore. It's purely lust."

One of his dark brows quirked. "Is that all?"

"Of course. I don't know you well enough for it to be anything else."

"That can be remedied. You still owe me a dinner."

No! Tess silently shouted while her eyes widened at the thought of spending any more time alone with him. In just under five minutes she had lost all rationality. What would happen if they spent a whole evening together? She didn't even want to think about that.

"Are you reneging on our deal?"

She felt trapped. Her gaze darted around the kitchen as if that would offer her a way out of her situation. "No, of course, not. Why don't you and your children come to dinner next Saturday night?"

"It's not going to work, Tess."

"What?" Her voice squeaked.

"The deal was for you and me to go out to dinner. No

children were mentioned. Remember a sit down place where you have to wait for your food."

"Okay. Then next Saturday it is." The cornered feeling intensified. "Now I do think it's time for us to go." She sidestepped around Zachariah and hurried toward what she hoped was Lance's bedroom.

She stopped in the doorway and watched Lance and Wesley together, their heads bent over an elaborate piece made of Legos. Lance was showing Wesley something he had built, pointing out every detail of the castle. Tess was impressed. Zachariah's son had a good sense of balance.

"Hi, Mom," Wesley said when he looked up and saw her. "See what Lance made. It took him a whole week." Her son pointed to the castle, awe on his expression.

"It's beautiful."

"He combined several of his big sets to make it. I think I'm going to do that, too." Wesley leaped to his feet, eager to get started. "You can come over when I get through," he said to Lance as he walked toward her.

Tess was happy that her son had finally invited someone over to the house, but why did it have to be Lance who was connected to Zachariah? She didn't want to be around him anymore than was necessary.

"Sure." Lance put a piece of Lego on top of the wall. "And don't forget about soccer practice tomorrow. Our team is called the Cimarron Devils. We could use another player since Tim broke his arm."

"Broke his arm? Playing soccer?" Tess asked, suddenly not sure of the wisdom in wanting Wesley to play the sport. Maybe he could join a chess team.

"No, Tim fell out of a tree." Zachariah answered, coming up behind her. "I hope you can come to practice, Wesley."

"I don't know," her son said, indecision in his eyes, his teeth gnawing on his bottom lip. "I might be busy tomorrow evening."

Zachariah laid his hand on Wesley's shoulder. "Have your mother bring you out to watch us practice."

Wesley looked up at Zachariah. "Maybe."

"I'll look for you both tomorrow," Zachariah said as Tess and Wesley left the house.

She would have liked to have shouted back at him, "No way," but this would be her son's decision. If he wanted to go and watch, she would go with him even though she didn't like feeling as if she were walking over hot coals.

It was the third week in September and Cimarron City was having a heat wave, Tess thought as she watched Zachariah out on the soccer field in a T-shirt and a pair of shorts that exposed way too much skin for her peace of mind. He should be clearly stamped with "If Partaken Too Long, Dangerous to a Woman's Libido."

She dragged her gaze away from the man and followed her son's progress along the sideline. For the first thirty minutes of the practice he had sat next to her on the bleachers, but now he was up and pacing, his attention glued to the boys on the playing field. Her heart ached at the hesitation and indecision she saw in Wesley's eyes. Ever since Brad had walked out on the family, her second son hadn't been able to make a decision and usually was too afraid to express an opinion. She had tried to get him to open up and tell her what was going on inside his mind, but he wouldn't. He would retreat further within himself but never far physically from her.

Zachariah jogged over to Wesley. "Want to join us in some drills?"

Her son glanced back at her, a touch of fear in his expression. Tess started to get up when he swung back around to Zachariah and said, "I don't know."

"I sure could use your help."

Staring at the ground, Wesley scuffed his right tennis shoe into the dirt over and over, making a hole.

"I need an assistant." Zachariah placed a hand on her son's shoulder. "Wesley, you don't have to do anything you don't want to do, but I think you would be great for the team."

Her son looked up at Zachariah, amazement on Wesley's face. "Really? You do?"

He nodded. "Will you help me? We have an odd number of players and we need to pair off. I need someone to work with Lance on this drill. Otherwise he won't have anyone to practice with."

"Okay," her son said after a slight hesitation.

While Wesley walked beside Zachariah out onto the soccer field, Tess tried to contain the expanding pressure in her chest before she fainted from lack of air. Another thread bound her to the man. He was good for Wesley and seemed to know just what to say to get results. She didn't want to feel grateful to him; she didn't want to feel anything toward him.

For the next thirty minutes Tess focused her total attention on her son running with the ball, passing it, slowly becoming a part of the team. For thirty minutes she succeeded in not looking at Zachariah and was quite proud of herself until a boy fell and hurt himself. She was drawn to the scene by the child's cries.

Kneeling by the boy, Zachariah checked out the child's cut on his knee and spoke soothingly to him the whole time. The injured team member sniffed and slowly began to listen to what Zachariah was saying. Tess couldn't hear, but whatever it was worked. The child grinned, shook his head and raced over to his partner in the drill, forgetting his cut. Zachariah had performed magic as if he had waved a wand over the boy.

For a brief moment Tess wished Zachariah could take her hurt away with some attention and a few soothing words. But the pain of rejection wouldn't heal that easily. Nor did she want to forget what happened to her. Brad's lesson had been a hard one, but she had learned it well. The only person she could depend on was herself.

"Mom," Wesley said, running up to her. "Did you see me kick the ball?"

"Yes." Tess rose, rolling her shoulders to work the stiffness from them. "I see you haven't forgotten anything from last year."

"Yeah." Her son's voice sounded amazed that he had remembered so much from playing soccer the year before.

"Well, what do you think, Wesley? Do you want to join us?" Zachariah asked, walking up behind the boy.

The uncertainty flittered across her son's features again, and Tess felt like crying. For every step forward there were two steps backward. "If you want we can come out and watch again tomorrow," she suggested.

"You can always do that, Wesley, but Lance and I would like to come by and pick you up for practice. How about it?"

While her son nodded, Tess felt shut out, unwanted. She started to make a comment about male bonding when Zachariah clapped Wesley on the back and said, "Great. I think you'll make a good forward."

At that moment Lance came up to Wesley and wanted him to meet some of the team members so before Tess realized it she was alone with Zachariah and fuming. "Don't build him up with false hopes," she said, suddenly wanting to protect Wesley from further hurt that had nothing to do with playing soccer and everything to do with Zachariah becoming too important in her son's life.

Zachariah sighed. "I would never do that, Tess."

"But he hasn't played much. He quit after Brad left."

"What happened?"

"Wesley didn't want to go to practice. No matter what

I did he wouldn't go. He would lie on his bed curled into a ball complaining that his stomach was hurting."

"I don't mean with Wesley, Tess. What happened with Brad?"

She drew herself up, tense. "Nothing."

She began to step around him when his hand shot out and clasped her arm. "You can't run forever."

"I'm not running. I don't know where you get your ideas. You make me sound like I'm a fugitive."

"I may be a cop, but I do know where to draw the line." The curve of his mouth cut into a frown.

"Do you? I feel like you're interrogating me."

"Because I want to get a little personal?" A nerve twitched in the hard plane of his jaw. "What did that man do to you to make you so scared to get close to anyone?"

Her own anger matched his. "None of your business." The words came out between clenched teeth. "I think it's time we go."

"Do you always leave when things get a little heated?"

If that were the case, she would have left an hour ago, she thought, remembering the hot feeling that suffused her body while she had watched the practice, or rather watched Zachariah. "Tomorrow is a work day. I have two other children—" she paused, inhaled in a deep breath and said, "I don't owe you an explanation."

"No, but what time do you want me to pick you up Saturday night?"

She blinked at the sudden change in the conversation. Oh, Lord! She had tried to put Saturday night from her mind. A date, she thought with mounting dread. "Seven."

"Do I dress up or go casual?"

How about in a suit of armor with your body covered from head to toe. "Casual."

"Where are we going?"

I don't know. Definitely some place crowded and noisy. "You'll find out Saturday night."

"Lady, you do love your secrets."

"I thought men liked women with a little mystery," she said and regretted the retort the minute she said it. She had a way of sticking both feet into her mouth without a backward glance.

His gray eyes widened, then his grin did. "Is that your game?"

"I don't play games."

"That's what I thought, too, until you said that." His eyes brightened with his smile.

"Sometimes I speak before I think."

"Not often enough. I still know little about you, Tess, but hopefully Saturday night will change that."

"Don't count on it. We're just going to dinner. Nothing else."

"But we do have to talk over dinner."

Not if I can help it. "It's not polite to talk with food in your mouth."

"And you plan on having food in your mouth the whole time?"

If it's possible. "I do like to eat."

"Ah, something personal. I think I'm making headway," Zachariah said, amusement deep in his voice.

Right into a brick wall, Tess thought, strengthening her resolve to keep this man at arm's length. She looked around him and motioned to Wesley to come to her. "It's getting late and this is a school night."

"We're all going to Braum's for some ice cream. Why don't you two join us?"

Her son came to a screeching stop next to her. His expression perked up when he heard the words ice cream. Her children had a thing about sweets, inherited honestly from her, and ice cream was at the top of their list.

She started to make her excuse not to go but realized she was placing her personal feelings ahead of her son. She would just make it a point to keep the thirteen boys on the team between her and Zachariah at Braum's. Surely she could manage that small feat.

Fifteen minutes later Tess knew the folly in her thinking. She had forgotten to factor in Zachariah's determination. Now she was sitting at a table in a corner with the man across from her. She didn't even have her son as a buffer. Somehow Zachariah had arranged for Wesley to sit at a table with several other boys including his son.

Officer Smith was a whirlwind, Tess thought, feeling as if he had swept into her life and mixed everything up until she couldn't tell what reality was. It was hard to resist his powerful aura. It was a challenge she was just as determined to win as he was.

"Never thought I would want to trade places with an ice cream cone," Zachariah said as he watched her lick hers.

She blushed. "Get your mind out of the gutter, Officer Smith. You're supposed to set an example for us."

An innocent expression wiped the sensuality from his features. "I was thinking about the heat. What were thinking about?"

She felt the color in her cheeks deepen. "You know lately the weather has been beastly." This was a neutral topic, she thought and continued, "Do you think we'll get rain soon? It's been almost four weeks since the last one."

"I'm not sure the rain would cool things off."

His gaze drilled into her with a relentlessness that stole her breath. She didn't need a neon sign to tell her the man wasn't thinking about the weather.

"And think of the humidity that accompanies rain. It cloaks you like wet silk. Every time you step outside you become drenched. I can't seem to shed enough clothes to get comfortable."

Okay, so the weather wasn't neutral enough. Next. "Violence on TV is awful. I spend half my time policing the programs my children watch. Do you have that trouble?"

Laughter danced in his eyes. "I find sex on TV even

worse than the violence. The other night I came in from putting Emily down and found Lance watching a movie. The two people were in bed, kissing and fooling around. After turning off the set, I spent fifteen minutes explaining the facts of life to my first grader."

Moving right along. "The national debt is atrocious. I have to balance my checkbook. Why can't Congress balance its checkbook?"

Zachariah covered her hand on the table with his. "I don't want to talk about the weather, television or the national debt. At this moment I don't care about those topics. The only one that interests me is you."

She was afraid of that. Her eyelids slid close. She felt the warmth of his fingers over hers and for a few seconds relished the feeling. When she finally looked at him, she drew her hand back, placing it in her lap. "Why?"

"Isn't it obvious?" One of his brows arched. "I want to be your friend, possibly more. I had a good marriage with Laurie. I like being in a relationship with a woman."

Every muscle in Tess's body stiffened at the words, marriage and relationship. She swiveled her chair around and bolted to her feet. "Good night, Officer Smith. I'll see you Saturday night."

With her son in tow, she couldn't get out of Braum's fast enough. She hurried to her car, aware that Zachariah was watching her through the plate glass window. She fumbled with the keys, dropped them, and had to pick them up. Once inside her car she took deep breaths after deep breaths, but her heart wouldn't stop pounding.

She didn't want a relationship and she certainly wouldn't marry again. And she would make that crystal clear Saturday night if it was the last thing she did.

Chapter Five

Tess opened the front door to find Zachariah standing there, wearing his jogging shorts and a tank top, holding a plastic measuring cup in his hand. "Aren't you a little early for our date? It's Friday."

He grinned and held up the cup.

"And I'd say you're a little too casual," Tess continued, trying to ignore the man's smile. "I'd promised you we weren't going to go to McDonald's."

"I need to borrow a cup of sugar."

"You jogged four blocks for a cup of sugar? The supermarket's only two blocks from your house."

"I need the exercise."

Tess swore to herself she wouldn't look down at his perfect built, but her eyes seemed to have a will of their own as they trekked southward, taking in his muscle bound chest, his flat stomach, his runner's legs. "Bull."

"Okay, I'll tell you the truth if you promise not to slam the door in my face and run away."

She sucked in a breath and held it, trapping his scent that teased her senses.

"I wanted to see you."

Her lungs burned and she released her pent up breath. Her grip on the door frame strengthened.

"I've missed you when I've come to pick up Wesley for practice."

She had deliberately been busy when Zachariah had come to the house to get her son. She had decided after the Braum's episode that was the only way to deal with the man. A room full of people didn't make her safe from his influence. "Just what are you gonna fix with the sugar?" Tess asked, not intending to get into a discussion that was personal.

"Fudge."

Her mouth watered at the thought of delicious chocolate loaded with calories and nuts. She knew the look on her face expressed her love for anything chocolate.

"You could help me make the fudge. I'd share it with you afterward. How about it?"

A picture of him feeding her a piece slipped unbidden into her thoughts like a thief into her house. Her mind swirled with the image.

He stepped closer. "Do you want to share, Tess?"

Through the haze that captured her mind, she heard the word share, a husky appeal that tilted the world even more for her. She shook her head, more to dislodge the vision of him sharing his fudge with her then to answer his question.

"For some reason that answer doesn't surprise me." He sighed, making a big production out of it. "Well, in that case, I hope I can at least have some sugar." With a big, silly grin on his face, he moved his eyebrows up and down. "No pun intended."

"I'm sure you didn't intend." Tess moved to the side

to allow Zachariah into the house, her grip still tight on the door.

He advanced to the threshold and peered inside. "Before I dare, where's Bruce?"

"With Shaun and Wesley in their room."

"Good." Zachariah strode into the house. "I haven't gotten over the last time he greeted me."

"Yes, Wesley told me about how Bruce launched himself at you and knocked you through the doorway. Is that why you honk now?"

"If I've learned one thing as a cop, it's that you can't be too careful."

"You don't have to be a cop to learn that lesson."

"Yes, you could probably give me a few on being cautious."

Tess turned at the kitchen entrance. She glared at him, her hands on her hips. "For someone who wants something, you sure have a funny way of endearing yourself to me."

All amusement fled his features. "You're damn right I want something from you and it sure the hell isn't sugar, at least not the kind that comes in a package. Why else would a man jog two extra blocks and doesn't know how in the world he's going to jog home with a cup full of sugar?"

A grin flirted with the corners of her mouth as she backed into the kitchen. "Walk."

"Walk?"

"Yes, you should walk home and hold the cup carefully."

His tension evaporated as he propped himself against the doorjamb. "You could always drive me home."

The idea tempted her for about one second. "I have three children to get to bed."

"I'll bring you some fudge tomorrow night."

He dangled a temptation that was impossible to resist. "I can't be gone longer than five minutes."

"No problem."

Tess took his measuring cup and filled it with sugar, then handed it back. "Promise?"

"You've got the keys. You're in control."

That innocent expression of his heightened her suspicion. In control? She doubted it, but she snatched up her purse and headed for the back door, amazed at the length she would go for a piece of chocolate.

"It still sounds okay. That's good," he said when she started the engine.

"Definitely since I can't afford to repair it. I still haven't paid off the last time and won't for a while."

"If you need any help, I—"

"No," she said quickly, then added, "thank you but I'm fine."

"Look, Tess, I know how expensive children can be."

"That's *my* problem." Her voice indicated the subject wasn't up for further discussion.

"Doesn't your ex help with child support?"

Tess clenched her jaw. Her hands grasped the steering wheel until her knuckles whitened.

"Never mind. You don't need to answer that one. Obviously he doesn't."

She slanted a look toward Zachariah. His face was set in a grim expression, his attention on the road ahead. The tension in the car thickened. They still had to get through tomorrow evening because she owed him a dinner. She wasn't sure how she was going to manage. He wanted to know too much about her and she didn't want to relinquish even a small bit of herself.

She would have missed his driveway if he hadn't spoken up. She wasn't even sure how she ended up on the right street, let alone in front of his house. She didn't turn the engine off but waited for him to climb out of the car.

Zachariah didn't. He turned toward her, his arm sliding along the back of the seat, his hand dangerously close to her. "Not all men are bastards like your ex. Not all men abandon their families."

The tension became palpable and hung in the air between them. She gritted her teeth so tightly that pain shot down her neck. "I wouldn't know about all men, only my husband and father." She stared straight ahead. "Now if you don't mind, I need to get home."

She counted a full, agonizing minute before he left. She didn't wait for him to walk up to his house. Throwing the car into reverse, she backed out of the driveway at a sedate twenty-five-miles-an-hour in two seconds flat.

Zachariah stood on his porch and watched her speed away. Every bit of information concerning Tess that he learned was like pulling a tooth with a set of pliers—painful, excruciatingly slow. But tonight he had discovered why she was so wary. Now all he had to do was build a foundation of trust and he suspected it would be brick by brick.

"Hi, come in. Mommie isn't ready yet," Katie said, then whirled about to go into the living room. She ran to the couch and plopped down as though waiting for Zachariah to have a seat next to her. "I'm supposed to keep you enter—busy until she's ready."

He eased himself down onto the sofa, leaning back against the cushion with his foil covered plate of fudge in his lap. The aroma of orange mingling with a *strong* scent of flowers permeated the room, but he couldn't find any in a vase. The interesting mix of odors intrigued him. He would have to ask Tess about them.

"How long will she be?" he asked when he discovered the little girl staring up at him.

Katie shrugged. "Don't know. She just got out of the shower. We had an accident earlier." She pointed to the plate in his lap. "What's dat?"

"Fudge. An accident? What happened?"

"I spilled Mommie's perfume." Katie stuck her thumb in her mouth. "It stinks." She waved her small hand toward a place behind a chair, her nose wrinkling. "Mommie wasn't too happy."

Zachariah could just imagine what happened. He was about to comment on the incident when he heard a commotion from the back of the house. He looked from the little girl to the doorway into the hallway just as Bruce came bounding into the room with a bra dangling from his mouth.

Tess was right behind the Great Dane, yelling, "Come back here with that." She slid to a stop inside the room, her gaze colliding with Zachariah's. "I didn't know you were here. You're—" she glanced down at her watch, "on time." Crimson flooded her cheeks as she grasped the gaping front of her short terry cloth robe and started backing out of the room.

Bruce lumbered over to Zachariah, dropped the bra at his feet and laved his face. "Good dog. That's enough." He pushed at the Great Dane and finally dislodged Bruce from his lap. When Zachariah looked around the dog to seek help from Tess, she was gone from the doorway. What in the world was he supposed to do with this hellhound? he asked himself as he continued to shove the big brute away, the squashed plate of fudge slipping off his lap to land on the couch next to him.

Bruce backed up into the coffee table while Zachariah held him off. Katie bounced off the couch, giggling, and threw her arms around the dog's neck. Bruce wagged his tail and cleared the table of the three magazines and the TV remote control.

"Why don't you take Bruce to your room?" Zachariah asked as he scooted to the side, his hand still securely fastened onto the dog's collar in case the Great Dane changed his mind and decided to become his close personal buddy again.

"Can I have some fudge?"

He was about to say if her mother said it was okay, then changed his mind. He wasn't beneath offering a reward if it would get the Great Dane out of his face. "Sure." Unwrapping the foil, he withdrew a flattened piece of fudge from the plate and handed it to Katie who immediately popped the whole thing into her mouth.

While the little girl led the big dog from the room, Zachariah wondered how much money it would take to build Tess a fence. He could get a few friends to help with the labor. Maybe he could convince the neighbors who bordered the yard to help with buying the lumber. Then all he had to do was persuade Tess to let him do it. Probably moving the Great Pyramid would be an easier feat.

He bent over and retrieved the bra from the floor. He held the flimsy piece of lace in his hand, rubbing the delicate material between his forefinger and thumb. Images of Tess taking a shower, of drying herself off, of getting dressed, flashed across the screen of his mind in vivid technicolor. Rising, he began to pace, energy surging through him. A finely-honed tension gripped him as he shook those pictures from his thoughts. He would never make it through the evening if he kept that fantasy going. He would be a basket case before the salad was served.

He heard someone coming. He quickly stuffed the bra into his pants' pocket, as though caught doing something wrong, and spun toward the entrance into the hallway, praying his sexual fantasy wasn't written all over his face.

But that was going to be a hard feat when she looked so sexy, Zachariah thought as he took in her long sleeved but short red dress that hugged her curves like a second skin. Her slender legs seemed to go on forever as he allowed his gaze to coast down her length. The leisurely trek produced a tightening in his groin.

The first thing Tess saw when she entered was Zachariah standing by a chair with a grin plastered on his face. Immediately she thought of how she had burst into the living room only five minutes before dressed in her terry cloth robe that left little to the imagination. After escaping back to her bedroom, she had set a record getting ready. She just wanted this evening over with before she flung herself into his arms and said, "Take me."

"Hi, you look great," Zachariah said, clasping the back of the chair near him.

As his gaze slowly traversed her body in an upward sweep, she felt the heat in her cheeks rivaling the color of her dress. Why had she chosen to wear something so revealing, to give in to the feminine side of her psyche? Chalk it up to a moment of madness, she decided. "How long have you've been waiting? I didn't hear the doorbell earlier."

"I didn't ring it. Katie opened the door before I had a chance to. But I haven't been here long. I had just arrived when—" he paused, his eyes taking on a silvery liquid look, "when you came after Bruce."

"At least I had on my robe," Tess said, laughter bubbling up in her. "That dog has a nasty little habit of stealing clothes if you turn your back on him for one second. I had everything I was going to wear lying on my bed." She glanced around the living room. "By the way where is Bruce?"

"He's with Katie in her room. I bribed her with a piece of fudge." Zachariah gestured toward the plate on the couch. "Your share is slightly mashed but still edible if Katie is any indication."

"Not really. She'd eat anything that's chocolate. Definitely my daughter has taken after me. I'd better hide the rest or she will have the whole plate cleared before you can say the word, no." Tess took the fudge into the kitchen and stashed it in her hiding place that her children hadn't managed to find yet.

As she reentered the living room, Tess remembered what had caused her mad dash out of her bedroom. She scanned the area, a frown wrinkling her brow. "Where's my—" She let her question fade into silence as her gaze linked with Zachariah's.

"Your bra?"

She nodded.

"Here." Zachariah actually looked sheepish as he withdrew the lacy bit of material from his front pants' pocket.

"Oh," Tess murmured as she watched the bra slowly appear in his large hand. She thought about him handling it and couldn't help the blush that returned.

Flustered, she snatched the piece of lace from his outstretched palm and looked about for a place to put it. Finally she opened her big purse and crammed it down into the bottom of the bag. She was seriously thinking of burning her favorite bra, not because she was a feminist but because she didn't think she could ever wear it again and not conjure up a picture of Zachariah touching it. The image was way too intimate and hinted at the difficulty that laid ahead for her this evening.

"We'd better go. Our reservations are for seven thirty." Tess snapped her purse shut.

"Reservations? Definitely not McDonald's then. Where are we going?"

"Molly Flanagan's."

Zachariah stared down at her for a full minute, then started laughing. "I should have known you'd pick a place like that."

"Whatever do you mean?" Grinning, she batted her eyelashes at him as she sailed past him out onto the porch.

"It's the noisiest, most crowded restaurant in town. The waiters don't know the meaning of leaving you alone. Privacy is unheard of at Molly Flanagan's."

"It is? I heard the food is excellent."

Zachariah opened the car door for her. "And you want

to keep your mouth full at all times. It's not going to work, Tess Morgan. Did I tell you I was a detective in Chicago?"

"I should have known. You have that interrogating bit down pat," she said when he sat behind the wheel and started the car. "Why aren't you one here?"

"The hours are too long. I'd get a case and it would consume me. With two kids to raise I can't afford to do that. I need to be there for them."

Tess remembered his comment about all men not abandoning their families and felt another thread wind around her and bind her to him. This man would never walk away from his children.

"Besides, the police force in Cimarron City is far different than in Chicago."

"What made you go to Chicago in the first place?"

"I wanted to try the big city, but I've decided you can't take the country out of me. I like a smaller town. I feel more human here. Why did you move here from New Orleans?"

"Granny Kime gave me an offer I couldn't refuse."

When she didn't elaborate, Zachariah asked, "What offer?"

"A roof over our heads. Have you been to Molly Flanagan's before?"

He chuckled. "Yes, twice."

"Did you enjoy it?"

"I don't think nearly as much as I will tonight. About New Orleans—"

"Oh, I see we're here already," Tess interrupted. "I'm looking forward to the food."

"Is that all?"

"The entertainment, too."

Twenty minutes later Tess knew for entertainment the juggling busboy and the singing waitress couldn't compare to the man sitting across from her at the most private table possible in the rowdy restaurant. How had he managed to secure the one table hidden from the rest of the patrons by a big potted plant? The bright lights were even dimmer in this corner, Tess thought as she scanned the large room, the noise level high with laughter and merriment.

After Zachariah gave their order to the waitress who in turn sang it back to them, he lifted his water glass, his gaze touching hers and making a mockery of her plan not to be affected by this man. "To a fun evening, Tess."

She somehow managed to raise her glass and click it against his. To a short evening. By the way had she told him she turned into a pumpkin at nine o'clock?

"How's your work coming along?" Zachariah asked as he put his glass on the table.

"Great. I'm enjoying it. In fact, the company will be sending me to a seminar in Oklahoma City for a few days next month." Tess ran her finger along the rim of her glass. "Of course, I haven't been away from the kids except when I was in the hospital having Katie and Wesley."

"They'll do fine."

"I'm not worrying about them, it's Granny Kime. In case you haven't noticed, my children can be a handful."

"Nah." Laughter glittered in the gray depths of his eyes. "If it will make you feel any better, I'll drop in and check on them. Besides, Wesley will have practice so that will give me a good reason to be around. Your grandmother will never know."

Tess wanted to tell him they could handle everything by themselves, but she wasn't the only one involved here. Granny Kime was seventy-five years old, and Tess had to think of her first, not her pride. "Don't bet on it. She's one sharp cookie, but I don't think she would mind the extra pair of hands."

"I just have one favor to ask."

"What?"

"Take your perfume with you. If I had to clean up that

kind of mess, I'm afraid the boys at the station would never let me live it down."

"Katie told you about that?"

"It was obvious. Just one good whiff and you knew something wasn't quite right. Flowers and orange definitely are an usual combination."

"The orange scent you smelled wasn't the perfume."

"What happened? Did the boys have a fight with oranges?"

Tess waved her hand in the air. "Nothing like that. At least not this time. I use different kinds of aromas for different kinds of effects. The orange scent is a sedative."

Zachariah chuckled. "Did you put it on after the perfume was spilled or before?"

"After. I had to do something. I really should have known something was up. Katie had been eyeing it for days. I noticed it was gone when I got out of the shower. It didn't take me long to figure out what happened. I heard a crash in the living room and knew my only bottle of perfume had bit the dust."

"What was it?"

"True Love by Elizabeth Arden."

"Interesting name."

"Well, I suppose it's better than Doomed Love or Unrequited Love."

"What a cynic you are."

"A realist. And you can't tell me you're a policeman and don't have a—more realistic outlook on life."

"Believe it or not I've not only seen the very worst in people but also the very best."

A man and their waitress approached them with their salads, making a big production out of serving them. Tess was sure everyone in the restaurant was watching as the couple, dressed like Romeo and Juliet, sang a love ballad at the end. Tess was thinking about moving the potted plant over several feet to block her totally from view as the pair finished with a bow and curtsy.

"They do like to call attention to us," Tess commented when they were alone again.

"They're just warming up."

"I was afraid of that." Tess stabbed a piece of lettuce with her fork. "You're enjoying every second of this."

"Yep. I figure by tomorrow it will be all over town we're an item." Zachariah surveyed the patrons, every table occupied in the large restaurant. "It looks like half the population of Cimarron City is here tonight. This is a very popular place and Saturday night at that."

The sparkle of laughter in his eyes infuriated Tess. She didn't want to be linked with him; she didn't want to be the object of people's gossip. She had had more than her share when Brad walked out on her and the children so suddenly. She could still remember the pitying looks she had received when she went to the grocery store or to Shaun's school.

The rest of the meal was like the salad course. The personnel of the restaurant had decided that Tess and Zachariah were the new couple in town and were making sure everyone else knew it, too. She must have heard every love song that had been written in the past fifty years. The next time she ever took someone out she would investigate the place before going to it.

As they were leaving Molly Flanagan's, a rubber suction cup arrow shot past Tess and stuck to the wooden door two feet from her. She glanced back to see a person dressed up as Cupid smiling at her and putting another arrow in his bow. Tess hurried out of the restaurant. She heard the thud as the door closed behind her and Zachariah. He laughed. She frowned.

"Do you think someone is trying to tell us something?" he asked as he drove out of the parking lot.

"No," she answered way too quickly.

"My favorite was the heart shaped piece of cake."

She looked at him without saying a word. Why couldn't they have been harassed like the people next to them? It had obviously been that man's fortieth birthday. The mortician and the nurse would have been a whole lot better than Rhett and Scarlet serving their main course.

When Zachariah pulled into the driveway and cut the engine, Tess heard the click of the lock on the doors. She pulled on the handle, but nothing happened. When she tried to unlock the door, she couldn't.

"Child proof," Zachariah said in answer to her unspoken question when she glared over at him.

"Well, unlock it. It's late. I have—"

He reached over and placed his fingers over her mouth. "Shh, Tess. Relax. It's only nine. I'll flip the lock open when you promise not to bolt the first chance you get."

It occurred to her that she should be afraid but she wasn't. She knew she would always be safe and protected with Zachariah. "Katie will probably still be up. She doesn't go down well unless I read her a bedtime story."

"What's a few extra minutes? I patiently sat through an hour and a half of singing, ribbing, dancing and juggling. The least you could do is sit for a while and talk. I'm starved for an adult conversation after spending all day with Lance and Emily."

"What do you want to talk about?" she squeaked, her heart starting to beat fast.

"Oh, we could try the weather, television or the national debt, but I think we've already covered those topics." He snapped his fingers. "Hey, I have a novel idea. How about you? We've barely touched that one."

She stiffened. She had learned painfully that when she let someone into her private world she opened herself up to be hurt. "You know all the important stuff."

"Do I? Why are you afraid to trust me?" He moved closer, his arm resting along the back of the cushion.

"I do. If I didn't I would be screaming right now."

"It's not the same thing. You know I'd never hurt you physically, but you think I will emotionally."

"If you already know the answer, then why bother asking the question?"

"Because there's much more to this, Tess."

Zachariah grazed his thumb down her cheek, the caress so soft she wondered if he had touched her at all.

"What did your ex do to you?"

She flinched back out of his reach. His probing questions demanded too much of her. "Open this door. Now."

Zachariah sighed heavily and threw the lock. As she bolted from the car, he was right behind her, his long strides matching her hurrying ones. Before she had a chance to escape into the house, he grasped her arm and whirled her to face him.

"What did your ex do to you?" He thrust his face close to hers, the silver glint in his eyes diamond hard.

"He left me. He was there one day and gone the next. He took everything with him. He cleaned out our savings and disappeared. He left me to explain to three children why their father didn't want them anymore. He left me to wonder how I was going to feed, clothe and care for them." Her chest rose and fell rapidly with each breath she dragged into her burning lungs. The pressure in her chest was tight, painful. "Are you satisfied? Now do you see why I don't trust easily?"

"Yes, finally we're getting somewhere." He pulled her over to the porch swing and pushed her down onto it. "Not everyone is like your ex and I'm going to prove that to you." He sat next to her, his arm about her shoulder.

Tess didn't pull away. She was too tired suddenly to do much of anything except stare straight ahead. All her suppressed anger toward Brad swamped her, threatening to shatter what composure she had left. One shudder then another rippled down her length.

Zachariah's hold on her tightened as he brought her up against his hard contours. His hand ran up and down her arm as though he were trying to warm her. "Have you tried to find your ex?"

"Try?" She could hear the hollow ring to her laugh. "When you have no money and little resources there isn't much you can do."

"I could help. I do have connections with the police."

"We've had this conversation before. I will make it on my own. I don't want Brad's help anymore. He walked out on us. He has no right to be apart of our lives now."

"Is that fair to your children?"

"Fairness went out the door the minute he left." Even though the night still held the heat of the day captured in the air, Tess felt cold. Shivering, she snuggled against Zachariah's warmth, knowing in one part of her mind the danger in doing that.

"Let me be your friend, Tess."

"Is that all you want?" A wariness, honed from betrayal, crept into her question.

"No, but I will be content with that if that's all you can give right now."

She didn't know what to say. In New Orleans she had had a few female friends but never a male one.

"I'm a good listener. Laurie taught me well. If you want to rant and rave about the problems of the day, I can take it."

This time her laugh was genuine. "That's an enticing offer."

"It was meant to be."

She placed her arm around him, seeking the comfort of his embrace. She needed a hug; it had been so long since she had had one. "Okay, but you must realize I don't have much more to give."

"Fine." He encircled her with both arms and held her

close as though he sensed her need and sought to fulfill it.

The sounds of the night floated to Tess as she sat holding Zachariah and feeling at peace. She heard a dog bark somewhere down the street. She saw a car pass the house. Life went on but for her she felt a shifting deep inside of herself. Since coming to Cimarron City, she had missed having someone to talk to. She had tried not to worry Granny Kime so Tess had kept things as light as possible with her grandmother. Maybe she could trust Zachariah to be her friend and give her the room she needed, Tess thought as she felt his even breathing, his steady heartbeat.

"Maybe this talking thing will work." Tess pulled away from him, allowing his arm to lie loosely about her shoulder. "I usually like to run when the little things in life become overwhelming, but it's becoming harder to run in the evening since the days are starting to get shorter. By the time I'm ready to exercise it's getting dark. I thought about running with Bruce, but frankly I don't relish chasing a dog around the park."

"Then let's do it together. I like to run, too. We'll arrange a time convenient for both of us and just do it. Great stress releaser."

"I usually can't until seven thirty or eight."

"That's okay. Nora has a daughter who can sit with the children while I run in the evening."

"Are you sure? I was beginning to think I would have to give it up or run alone in the dark, something I never would have considered in New Orleans."

"Yes, I'm sure, Tess. With soccer practice two days a week it's becoming harder for me to do it earlier. And I don't want you to run alone." He tugged her to him and put the swing in motion.

She heard the protective ring to his last sentence. "The park is well lit and this is Cimarron City not New Orleans," the imp in her said.

His foot came down to stop the swing. He straightened and stared down at her. "Promise me you won't ever do something foolish like that. I've been a policeman too long not to be concerned."

"This is a passionate subject for you?"

"You're damn right it is. When I was a rookie, part of my territory was the park. One summer there was a rapist who attacked young women jogging in the evening. He used a knife on them." Zachariah gripped her upper arms, bringing her close. "Just promise me."

She nodded, surprised she wasn't upset at his highhandedness.

"Good." He relaxed back. "I'll pick you up at eight tomorrow night then."

Tess couldn't believe the evening was ending with them making plans to see each other almost every day to run. She knew she certainly needed a running partner. She had vowed earlier to sever ties with Zachariah and now she was tied to him even more than before. Surely she could control her physical reaction to the man. She hoped she knew what she was doing.

Chapter Six

Zachariah stood in Tess's doorway with Emily in his arms and Lance behind him, a pine scent that permeated the house beguiling his senses. He drew the aroma deep into his lungs and felt more relaxed. "Are you sure about this, Mrs. Kime? Tess and I don't have to run tonight if you have any doubts."

"Young man, I'm sure. I don't offer to do something I don't want to do. Now you two run along."

"Granny Kime, that's rich. Run along, Mom. I'm gonna show Lance my Lego sets." Wesley motioned to Zachariah's son to follow him.

Zachariah placed Emily on the floor with the diaper bag. Before he had a chance to turn toward the door, Katie came up to Emily, took her hand and led her away. He paused, still not sure he and Tess should go to the park. He looked toward her with a question in his gaze.

"They'll be okay. Shaun's studying in my room. Wesley and Lance will play with Legos and won't even know we're gone," Tess said, offering a smile even though at the moment she still felt wrung out. She inhaled deeply of the pine-scented air and let the aroma soothe her, but even its effects weren't working as she wished.

"They aren't the ones I'm worried about." Zachariah watched while Katie started walking around the living room with Emily in tow.

"You can't touch dis. Dat's off limits." Katie pointed to two objects on the bookcase, then moved to an end table to continue her dictates.

Tess clasped Zachariah's hand and pulled him out the door. "Katie told me she wanted to show Emily her toys in her room. She's been dying to play house all day and Emily has been elected to be her daughter. It's only an hour."

"Tess, you and I both know all that can happen in an hour's time. For that matter in five minutes' time."

She opened the door to his van. "I need this. Believe me Granny Kime wouldn't have agreed if she didn't want to. She told me once she was too old to do anything unless it suited her."

He started the engine, then glanced at her. "Are you sure you're up to this? You look tired."

"Gee, thanks," she said with a laugh that felt good. "Tired isn't the right word. Stressed is more like it."

"I have to admit you have the most interesting smelling house. Obviously that is what a pine aroma relieves."

Tess's eyes widened. "Why, yes. When you had a day like I did you will do almost anything to combat the stress."

"What happened?"

"I had a conference with Wesley's teacher again today. You know a few weeks back my son was too quiet and withdrawn in the classroom. Well, now he is too disruptive and actually aggressive on the playground. He got into a fight with a boy during recess. He bloodied his nose and made the boy cry. He is suspended for the rest of the week. A first grader!" The tension she had felt since the meeting intensified. Tess rolled her shoulders and rubbed the back of her neck.

"Lance did mention it."

"I don't understand what's going on with that child. I can't believe I actually miss the child he was a month ago. He comes out of his bedroom now, but all he does is fight and get upset at everyone. Thank goodness he and Lance are becoming friends. Maybe your son's influence will settle him down."

"Do you want me to talk with Wesley? See what's bothering him?"

"No," came automatically out before Tess had time to think. Then she remembered the last time he had wanted to help with Wesley and quickly added, "I appreciate the offer but he's my son. I need to have that talk with him. I've tried but obviously not hard enough." Offering to help was as much a part of Zachariah as his heart was. She couldn't accept that kind of assistance, just as obviously he couldn't accept the word no.

He pulled into a parking space at the park. "We'll run an extra lap. Maybe that will help."

Tess climbed from the van and immediately started stretching. "Since we started running regularly, things seem easier to deal with. I've always known exercise is good for stress, but without someone to do it with, it was easy not to run when something little interfered."

"Yeah, when someone else is miserable right along with you, it is so much better." He placed his left leg on the bumper of his van and bent over, touching his foot and holding the position.

"Right. When I'm about ready to give up, you force me to go an extra lap or two."

He bowed. "Simon Legree at your service. Ready?"

"Not just yet. I'm really tight tonight."

Tess felt Zachariah's gaze on her as she finished up her last series of stretches. Under the light of the street lamp, she could see the golden cast to his hard features. On the cool breeze she could smell his particular scent of musk and her body responded with a faster beat of her heart as if she had completed several laps.

While she twisted from side to side, she thought back over the past three weeks. Every evening that the weather had been decent they had run and talked. She knew everything about him. And she liked what she knew. She had even found herself "ranting and raving" when she had needed to because something hadn't gone right that day. He would listen, sometimes offer his help as was his nature. Brad had never listened, had always told her what he thought then stormed away. And above all had never supported her. It was nice to have someone to talk to besides her family and have her feelings validated.

"I'm ready now," Tess announced when she realized her body was beginning to react to him watching her with a sexual tightening in the pit of her stomach.

Zachariah set a grueling first three laps, and Tess thought she wasn't going to make it. But by the time she started on the fourth one the earlier stress melted away, leaving in its wake a calm acceptance. Wesley was moving through moods. Perhaps this recent anger was closer to what he was feeling than his passiveness of the past year. If so, then what was happening was good. Hopefully before long he would open up and tell her what was bothering him. She felt it went much deeper than Brad walking out on them.

When they completed their five miles, they walked around in circles to cool down. With her breathing evening out, Tess stopped finally and stared up at the dark sky. She found the first star and made a wish that Wesley would be all right, that she wouldn't have a juvenile delinquent on her hands at the ripe old age of six.

Zachariah came up behind her and leaned close to her ear. "I hope it comes true."

She whirled about and stepped back. "What do you mean?"

"Your wish."

"How did you know?"

"Lucky guess. You were looking at that star for so long I knew something was going on. Care to tell me what your wish was?"

"No way, Zachariah Smith. You know better than to even ask."

He shrugged. "You can't blame a guy for trying."

"And you have that down." Tess began walking toward the van. "You are one persistent guy."

"Help. Stop that man," a woman shouted.

Alert and tense, Zachariah scanned the parking lot and saw two women pointing toward a man near a car. He spun about, caught sight of Zachariah, and ran toward the trees.

Zachariah tossed the keys to Tess. "Use my car phone. Call the station." Then he took off after the man, pausing briefly to make sure the women were all right.

With her hands shaking, Tess placed the call to the police, the whole time her gaze pinned on the area where Zachariah had disappeared through the trees. Her heart raced as though she hadn't finished running and couldn't catch her breath. What if the man had a gun? What if Zachariah got hurt?

After informing the police, she walked over to the two women. "Are you all okay?" Tess asked, her voice steadier than she felt. A picture of Zachariah wrestling the man to the ground, a knife poised between their bodies, flashed into her mind.

"That man was trying to steal my car," the taller of the two women said. "We just bought it two months ago."

"Who was that?" the other asked, pointing in the general direction of the trees.

"Zachariah Smith. He's a policeman," Tess answered, grasping on to that thought. He was trained to take care of a situation like this, she told herself while the seconds slowly ticked away.

"Carolyn, I told you we shouldn't have come to the park so late." The short one frowned.

"But this is Cimarron City. Hunter's Park has always been safe." Carolyn rubbed her hands up and down her arms. "I can't believe this is happening. Thank goodness Officer Smith was here. That man could have killed us."

Tess's eyes grew round, her fear mushrooming. "Killed you? Did he have a gun?"

"Well, no, not that I saw," Carolyn answered. "But the man was so big."

Tess couldn't have thought her heart could beat any faster but it was. She felt as though it would explode any second. The sight of flashing red lights, the sound of the policemen's car doors slamming shut, comforted her only a small bit. What finally caused her heartbeat to begin to return to its normal rate was the sight of Zachariah coming toward her from the trees. He had the thief secured with both arms behind his back.

Relief fluttered through her like the wings of a hummingbird against a glass cage. Her legs felt so weak she wanted to sink to the ground. She realized what Zachariah had done that evening really had nothing to do with him being a policeman and everything to do with the man he was. He didn't let a little thing like fear stand in his way.

Carolyn hurried up to Zachariah after the two policemen relieved him of his suspect. "Oh, Officer Smith, you were so great. Thank you. Thank you. My husband would have been furious if anything had happened to his car."

The short woman rushed over to her friend. "I want to thank you, too. My purse was on the floor."

"You're welcome, ladies. But next time leave your purses at home. That may have been what he was attracted to." Zachariah looked up, his gaze connecting with Tess's. "Now if you'll excuse me, I must be going."

The muscles in her stomach tightened as he walked toward her. He looked wonderful to her eyes. His strides were long and purposeful. The expression on his face twisted her insides into knots. Instantly a sexual tension sprung up between them, and she wished they were any place but the park.

"Let's go." He took a hold of her arm and practically dragged her toward the van.

Silence ruled on the drive to her house, but Tess noticed the white knuckle grip of his fingers on the steering wheel and she felt the tension in the air heighten. He was wound tightly.

When they arrived at Granny Kime's, he reached over and clasped her arm to keep her from leaving even though she hadn't made a move to open the car door. Before she knew it, he pulled her toward him and his mouth descended on hers, his tongue thrusting its way inside.

She felt the energy and tension bottled up inside of him expand and flow through her. All resistance she might have had evaporated like the dew on a hot summer's day. Winding her arms around his neck, she angled herself to fit more securely against him.

His kiss was hot and fierce like the emotions rampaging through him. While she was swept along in the intensity of his possession, he pushed her back until she was half lying on the seat. With his lips devouring hers, he slid his hand under her T-shirt, moving upward, grazing over her skin in a light touch that sent rocket-like sensations shooting through her.

When he cupped her bra clad breast, she moaned and completely forgot where they were. When he trailed a nibbling path to her ear and bit on its lobe, she swam in a sea of delicious tingles. When his harsh breathing bathed her ear and neck as he moved lower, she clutched at his shoulders as if holding on to him would keep her from drowning in his fervent emotions that were quickly becoming hers.

He hit something and jerked. "Oh, damn. This isn't the right time or place," Zachariah muttered as he pulled back from her, his body looming over hers partially stretched out on the front seat.

Slowly her senses returned, and Tess remembered they were in her driveway. A blush crept up her face. She felt like a teenager necking in a car. The only thing missing was a policeman coming along and shining a flashlight into the window. Or worse, five kids peeking into the van.

Tess scooted up against the door while she tugged down her T-shirt. She could hear the sound of their labored breathing. She could taste him still on her lips. She could smell him as if he cloaked her in his essence. And she could see the silver glitter of passion in his eyes as she pushed the door open and the interior light came on.

She needed fresh air. She needed the safety of the house and the six people inside. She needed to get away from Zachariah before she did something totally irrational and against everything she had planned for in the future.

"Wait, Tess," he called out when she placed her foot on the first step.

A part of her resisted the temptation to turn around, but that traitorous part that responded to him in a blink of an eye slowly faced him as he trotted toward her.

"I'm not sorry about what happened, but I am sorry about the timing, Tess." He stopped nerve rackingly close.

She backed up the steps. "That's okay. I understand."

"Do you?"

"My adrenaline was pumping, too, after that scene in the park."

He mounted the stairs, still too near for comfort. "That was part of it, but for the past few weeks every time I have seen you kissing you is all I can think about. You're one dynamite lady, Tess Morgan."

She didn't want to talk about herself; she didn't want to talk about his kisses, his feelings. "And you can certainly take care of yourself. That man had a hundred feet on you."

"I run for pleasure. He doesn't."

Her laugh came out shaky. "I don't know if I call running pleasurable."

"I do when I have a partner like you."

His words fluttered her heartbeat. She continued to move backward toward the door, and he continued to match each of her steps with one of his own until she was plastered against the screen. He bracketed her head with his arms and leaned into her.

"There will come a time and place that is just right," he whispered close to her mouth.

"I thought you wanted to be my friend."

"I do. I am."

"This isn't in my definition of what a friend does."

"It is in mine. Laurie and I were best friends as well as husband and wife—lovers."

Tension whipped through her like a cat-o'-nine-tails lashing at her nerve endings.

"Being friends doesn't exclude other kinds of relationships, Tess."

His breath tickled her lips. She pinched them together to wipe away any sensations he produced. It didn't work. She felt him as if he were the very clothes next to her skin.

"I am not going to hurt you."

She didn't think it was possible for him to get any closer, but he did. His mouth feathered across hers once then twice, and she couldn't come up with one thing to say to him.

"That's the furthest thing from my mind." He nipped at her lower lip and tugged on it.

As Tess felt herself sink into him, the porch light flashed

on. He jumped back as she wrenched to the side. The door flew open.

"Mom," Shaun said, pushing the screen wide. "I've finished my homework. Can I watch TV?"

She would have agreed to just about anything at that moment. "Yes, that's fine," she replied, praying that her son didn't hear the quavering sound in her voice, then added because she finally remembered she was a mother, "But only for an hour. It's a school night."

She quickly followed Shaun into the house with Zachariah right behind her. She felt his masculine presence down the length of her back. Perspiration coated her upper lip and forehead that had nothing to do with the heat or their run earlier.

"One of my qualities as a detective was I never gave up while chasing down a lead in a case," he murmured next to her ear.

She glanced back over her shoulder. "There's always a first time for everything."

"I hate to drop this interesting subject, but don't you think it's awfully quiet for five kids to be in the house? Do you think they tied up your grandmother and are plotting as we speak?"

"You may have a point. You check Wesley's room. I'll check Katie's."

Tess opened the bedroom door and found Granny Kime sitting in the rocking chair knitting while Katie was standing over Emily. One of her daughter's hands was on her hip while she was shaking the other at the baby. "No. No. No, you can't do that," Katie said in her sternest voice that Tess could have sworn sounded just like hers. "No chocolate ice cream for you for a whole year."

Tess exchanged a knowing smile with her grandmother. To Katie that was the worst possible punishment while to Emily all she heard were the words, ice cream.

The baby lumbered to her feet. "Want ice seam."

"I'm afraid you've got a rebellion on your hands," Tess announced to her daughter as Emily made her demand again but this time louder.

"Can we have some?" Katie asked, her eyes round with anticipation, while she licked her lips.

"If I didn't know better, I'd think you planned this, young lady."

"Want ice seam." Emily raced toward Tess. "Pick up."

Tess scooped the baby up into her arms and hugged her. It felt good to hold her. "I'll see what we have."

In the kitchen Tess checked the freezer and discovered a carton still half full, a small miracle in her household. She dished up two bowls for the girls and sat them at the table with Emily in Tess's lap.

Zachariah found them a few minutes later and laughed. "I'm not sure who got the most ice cream, you or Emily," he said to Tess.

She looked down at her shirt with chocolate stains all over it. "It's definitely a toss up. I started out letting her feed herself. A mistake as you can see. Thank goodness this is old and will now be a rag."

"If it's one thing I've learned with Emily, it's to wear old clothing when feeding her. I've thought about coming up with a plastic body suit that can be wash down along with the baby. Maybe I could make my fortune." Zachariah took his daughter from Tess's lap and walked to the sink.

"How are the boys? Any casualties?"

"It depends on what you mean by casualties. Now if you mean, are the boys fine, then no casualties. But if you mean the room and the Lego sets, then there are some mighty big ones."

"The room? The Legos?" Tess started to get up from the table, picturing the chaos in her mind.

"Don't worry. I've got them cleaning the mess up."

"You left them and you think they will?"

"You gotta remember I'm their soccer coach. They don't want to run laps tomorrow at practice."

Tess relaxed back in the chair. "I never thought to use that threat."

"Hang around me and I'll give you all sorts of tricks." Zachariah stripped off Emily's shirt and wiped down her face, arms and hands while the eighteen month old squirmed.

Tess came over to the pair and tried to distract Emily's attention from climbing down off the counter top. The child was having none of it. She wanted down and instantly. Finally when Zachariah had most of the chocolate ice cream cleaned off Emily, he lifted her to the floor and watched as she raced over to Katie.

"More," Emily said as she tugged on the four year old's arm.

Katie looked at Tess. "Can we, Mommie?"

"No, you all may not."

Emily stopped tugging and glanced back at the adults, her lower lip sticking out in fine pout. "More ice seam." Her voice rose several levels.

Zachariah snatched his daughter up into his arms. "We'd better go. She's about to erupt."

"Go on and take her home. I'll bring Lance to your house when the boys are through cleaning the bedroom."

"Good idea," Zachariah said as he hurried toward the front door while Emily began to cry. "I guess she's had too much excitement. See you tomorrow night."

Emily wasn't the only one who had had too much excitement for one evening, Tess thought as she watched Zachariah and his daughter leave. The sounds of Emily's wails could be hear from inside the house even with the van windows rolled up.

"He forgot his diaper bag," Granny Kime said as she walked up behind Tess at the screen door. "The girls and boys played well together. Everyone was quiet until the end. Isn't it nice they all get along?"

"Yes, nice," Tess murmured, concerned that Zachariah and Emily would be all right. "I'll have Lance take the diaper bag home when I take him."

"Why don't you? I'll make sure Katie and the boys get to bed on time. Take your time. You don't have to rush back home."

"It won't take me five minutes," Tess said with such a finality that she was even surprised by her tone of voice.

"He's getting to you, isn't he?"

"He's only a friend, Granny. Nothing more."

"I never kissed my friends like you kissed him."

Embarrassment fired Tess's cheeks. "That won't happen again."

"If you say so, my dear." Granny shuffled toward the kitchen and Katie.

It wouldn't if she could manage to stay away from parked cars, dark places, and where it was just him and her, Tess thought and closed the front door.

The front door slamming shut alerted Tess. The sound of pounding feet racing toward her brought her to her own feet. Wesley tore into her bedroom with a look of horror on his face and tears streaking down his cheeks.

"Bruce is gone. He ran off."

"What do you mean he's gone? How did he get out of the house?"

The tears intensified, making it difficult to understand Wesley. "I wanted—I wanted to take him for a—a—a walk." He drew in short gasps of air and hiccupped.

Tess knelt in front of her son and clasped his arms to get his full attention. "It's okay. Take deep breaths, honey, and then tell me slowly what happened."

"I put Bruce on his leash to walk him," Wesley said after

he had inhaled several times. "Bruce saw another dog and began to run after it. I couldn't hold on, Mom. I tried." He hiccupped again and sniffed. "Really, Mom, I did."

"Okay," Tess said very slowly. "Where were you when this happened?"

"Two blocks over. I was walking Bruce to Lance's." Tears still glistened in Wesley's eyes.

Tess rose and took her son's hand. "He's probably making his way home right now. We'll go out looking for him. It's hard to lose a dog as big as Bruce. He can't hide very well."

Two hours later Tess wished that what she had said was true, but after searching thoroughly for seven blocks, Bruce was nowhere to be found. A few people she had talked to saw the Great Dane chasing after another dog and would point in the direction he went. But when she and Wesley investigated, there was no sign of Bruce, only more rumors.

"Honey, we need to go home and get the car. Besides, maybe Bruce is already there."

The tears returned to streak down Wesley's face. "It's all my fault. He's gone. We'll never see him again."

Tess squeezed her son's hand. "We don't know that. There's still a lot of places to look."

When they arrived back at the house, Zachariah and Lance were sitting on the porch swing. Lance was dressed in his soccer uniform and for the first time Tess noted that Wesley was, too. Her son had missed the Saturday afternoon game.

"I was worried when Wesley didn't show up. What's the matter?" Zachariah asked as Tess and her son mounted the steps to the porch.

"Bruce got loose and we can't find him. We've been looking for two hours. We came home to get the car."

"Where is everyone? Out looking?" Zachariah pushed off the swing and strode to Tess.

She shook her head. "Shaun's at Freddie's for the day. Katie went with Granny to see a friend."

"Then I'll help you search. Where have you been?"

"Seven blocks that a way." Tess pointed in the direction they had looked.

"That's toward the park. I'll start where you stopped and head for it. I'll call the station to see if anyone has lodged a complaint about a big dog running loose. Someone's bound to see him and hopefully has reported it." Zachariah turned to Wesley. "Don't worry. We'll get him back. You and your mom should stay here just in case Bruce returns. Lance'll tell you about the game while you're waiting."

"Did we win?" Wesley asked.

Zachariah nodded.

"Please find my dog," Wesley said, a catch to his voice.

"I have some buddies who can help with the search for Bruce. I'll have him back here before dark."

"I'm the one who should be out looking," she said after the boys went inside the house. Suddenly she felt powerless.

"Someone should be here, Tess. Let me help you." Zachariah took her hand. "People need people. That's part of life."

"I don't have a choice in this case. If anything happened to Bruce, Wesley would be devastated. He's gone through too much in the past year. Please find him."

Zachariah lifted her hand to his mouth and kissed the back of it. "See that wasn't so bad." He gave her a brief smile. "I'll be back soon with Bruce."

For the next hour Tess paced, occasionally going inside to check on the boys who were talking in Wesley's bedroom. Tension began to pound against her brow as she went from one end of the porch to the other.

She didn't call out to Wesley and Lance when she saw Zachariah turned onto the street because she was afraid he hadn't found Bruce. But the instant he pulled into the driveway, the boys shot out of the house and raced for the van. Relieved to see the Great Dane in the back, Tess sagged against the railing while her son threw open the door and bounded inside. Thankfully Zachariah had a hold of the leash or there could have been a repeat of earlier.

"You found him. You found him," Wesley yelled.

"I'd better take Bruce into the house," Zachariah said as he slid from the van.

As he came up the steps, Wesley was right behind him, her son's hand on the Great Dane's back. After the dog was securely in the house and taken off the leash, Wesley threw his arms around Zachariah's waist.

"Thank you, Mr. Smith. I thought I would never see him again."

"Nonsense. You can't lose a dog like Bruce."

"Where was he?" Tess asked, her throat closing at the sight of her son looking up at Zachariah with worship in his eyes.

"At the park. He gave me a merry chase. He thought I was playing with him."

"He doesn't get to run like he should." Tess watched as the boys left her and Zachariah alone in the living room, taking Bruce back to Wesley's bedroom. She wanted to call out to them to come back and chaperon her, but they would have looked at her as if she had grown a second head. She bit back her words and took several steps away from Zachariah.

"You need that fence you were talking about earlier."

"Yes, but it's just not possible right now." Her tension headache hammered against her eyes. "Excuse me. I'll be right back."

She walked into the kitchen and retrieved her bottle of rosemary essential oil. After dabbing some onto her temples, she rubbed it into her skin.

"What's that for?"

Zachariah's question startled her and she spun about to face him. "I have a headache. This helps relieve it."

"Here let me." He removed her fingers and began to massage her temples.

Her eyelids drifted closed as he worked his magic. She felt the tension drain from her and didn't know if she should contribute it to the rosemary or his touch. She swayed toward him, her legs suddenly weak.

"I think I could get into this aromatherapy," he whispered, his mouth brushing across her ear. "I like this."

So did she and that was the problem, Tess thought as she forced herself to back away. "I'm fine now."

He looked disappointed but didn't say anything while she put the bottle back on the shelf where she kept her oils. She was aware of his gaze as it tracked her movements, making her hands shake. Another kind of tension gripped her as she faced him again.

He lounged against the kitchen table with his arms folded across his chest, his gaze intent upon her. "How about that fence?"

"I can't afford it. I wish I could but I can't."

"If there was a way—"

"But there isn't. End of story." Tess felt the room closing in on her as though Zachariah were stealing all the fresh air. She headed for the porch. Outside she inhaled deeply, but the sexual tautness that held her didn't recede.

"I need to pick up Emily before Nora thinks I'm lost," Zachariah said as he came out onto the porch.

"Let Lance stay. I'll bring him home after dinner." She infused her words with a stiff politeness.

"Very well," he said in an equally courteous voice as if they had never shared several kisses.

Tess refused to watch him leave, afraid all the emotions she was experiencing would be reflected on her face. She wanted him so badly and yet knew the pain that need would inflict. She would not go through that ever again, she vowed as she opened the screen door to go inside.

Chapter Seven

"Look at my son. Billy just made another goal. That's seven so far," the mother next to Tess said to her. "This is definitely a one-sided game."

Silently Tess agreed with a score of ten to zero, but she wasn't going to say anything to encourage the woman to expound on her son's soccer capabilities. Tess had already heard the child's brief, and according to his mother, exciting sporting history and could probably recite it as well as the lady.

"Now which one is your son?" the star player's mother asked.

Tess pointed to Wesley standing in the goalie box, scuffling his feet, kicking up dust around him, his gaze fixed upon something on the ground in front of him.

"Oh, yeah, that one," the woman said as though Wesley wasn't very memorable. "No wonder he's daydreaming. He's not getting much action and he probably won't."

Tess watched the "thundering herd" move as one around the field, most of the players on both teams going after the ball in a large group. Wesley and a fullback, who was picking a wildflower, were the only children holding their position. Everyone else was a forward with little Billy the most aggressive of the bunch, therefore the one who scored the most. Definitely the child took after his mother, Tess thought as the lady jumped to her feet and screamed so loud at her son that Tess was sure her hearing would never be the same.

Suddenly a player on the opposing team broke away from the pack and charged down the field toward Wesley. Tess looked toward her son and immediately swallowed her words of encouragement. Wesley was climbing on the net, his gaze now riveted on something near the top of the bar. A butterfly spread its wings and took flight.

Zachariah shouted from the sideline to get Wesley's attention. Finally he stared at the opposing player, heading straight for him. The fullback was still bent over looking at the grass. Quickly Wesley tried to untangle himself from the net and couldn't. His foot got caught in a hole.

"Can't have the goalie sleeping on the job. You should have a word with your son," Billy's mother muttered. "This will ruin our shutout."

Anger shot through Tess, and it took all her willpower not to knock the woman off the bleachers. Instead, Tess stood, and with her breath held, watched helplessly as her son struggled to pull his foot loose. She knew she would make it worse if she ran out onto the field and helped her son free himself but the urge was strong.

The "thundering herd" passed the parents in the stands. The lone player ahead of the swarm came toward Wesley, nearer and nearer. The fullback finally looked up and saw the mass of boys charging down the field. He ran forward to meet the opposing player and went right past him into the advancing mob. Wesley was now the only one who could stop the other team from scoring.

"Some kids shouldn't play the game," the woman next

to Tess said loud enough for everyone in the bleachers to hear.

Tess balled her hands at her sides as Wesley yanked his foot out of the net and scrambled toward his position. The opposing player stopped in front of the goalie box, brought his leg back, then swung it forward, connecting squarely with the ball. It sailed through the air as Tess felt her lungs ache from holding her breath so long. Wesley jumped up and punched the ball out. A cheer erupted around Tess as she clapped and yelled.

She sat back down, her chest puffed out with pride. "Now that was a beautiful save and we still have that all important shutout. After all, this game is paramount in the scheme of things. At this very moment there are probably college scouts out here watching for the next Pele. You just never know, so I say you should always be prepared in soccer. Or, is that the boy scouts?" Tess gathered up her purse and moved two rows down and to the left, leaving Billy's mother with her mouth hanging open.

From behind her Tess heard the woman say, "Well, I never," then huff.

The lady Tess was now sitting next to laughed. "Thank you. I've been wanting to tell her off myself. I'm Jane Pennington."

"I didn't think I could take another second of listening to her son's virtues. According to her the rest of the team should just sit on the sidelines and watch him play and learn from his marvelous moves." She stuck her hand out to shake with Jane's. "I'm Tess Morgan."

She enjoyed the rest of the game with Jane next to her, but Tess was relieved when it was over. This was the first time her son had played goalie. She didn't know if she liked the whole game resting on Wesley's shoulders. His ego was fragile. If he hadn't punched the ball out the time his foot got caught in the net, he would have been devastated. The next team could have more attempts on the goal and Wesley might not be so lucky.

"Mom, did you see my save?" Wesley raced up to Tess after the coaches had talked to the team.

"Sure did. It was a beauty."

"Yeah, Mr. Smith thought so to. I'm gonna be the goalie next week. Mr. Smith thinks I'll make a great goalie."

But what was going to happen when Wesley didn't make the save, Tess thought, remembering how he had quit doing anything competitive the past year, withdrawing further and further into his shell.

"Mr. Smith wants to work with me some extra. He's gonna talk to you about it at McDonald's."

"Then we'd better get going. I see the other boys already leaving."

"Can I ride with Mr. Smith and Lance?"

"I don't think—"

"Please, Mom. Wesley asked. Mr. Smith said it was okay. Please."

Her son gave her his pleading look and she couldn't say no. She nodded, feeling abandoned for Mr. Smith. As she walked to the car alone, Tess thought over the past few weeks. Besides Wesley's shift in behavior she realized he was also increasingly mentioning Zachariah's name in his conversations. Mr. Smith says this. Mr. Smith thinks this. Mr. Smith does this. Mr. Smith can do no wrong. There could be a worse problem brewing than her child's fragile self-esteem being hurt. What would happen when Mr. Smith was no longer in Wesley's life? What would happen when he walked out like Brad did?

At McDonald's Zachariah was waiting for her when she pulled into the parking lot. Wesley and Lance were already out on the playground. She remembered the sexual frustration she had felt the last time they had been alone together and thanked her lucky star that she wouldn't be by herself with the man.

"Hello," Zachariah said as she strode up to him.

The sensual gleam in his eyes made her wary. Somehow he always managed to make her feel they were the only two people in the world even though they were in the midst of a crowd. His smile produced a tightening in the pit of her stomach. This time was going to be no different. She could feel him working his magic already. He was stripping away her layers of protection.

"Hi." She moistened her dry lips with the tip of her tongue.

His gaze trekked her movement as though he wanted to devour her. She felt the energy drain from her legs and hoped she could make it inside without clutching him for support. It wasn't fair that a simple look, a simple greeting, could be so lethal to her.

"I've got the kids orders. What do you want?" Zachariah asked, his hand settling at the small of her back as they entered the restaurant.

For him not to be so wonderful, she thought, wishing the feel of his fingers on her didn't feel right. "Iced tea." Better yet, bring her a bucket of ice to stick her head in, Tess silently added as he walked up to the counter to give their orders to the teenager. She didn't think it was possible to be going through the change of life this early, but these hot flashes that kept blanketing her when she was around Zachariah sure were annoying.

Tess watched him while he talked with the young man behind the counter. Zachariah obviously knew the teenager. They exchanged more than the orders. When Zachariah approached Tess with the tray full of their food and drinks, he was grinning.

"I know we won today, but you're smiling as though you won the lottery," Tess said, feeling her body responding to his smile.

"It's just about as good. John," Zachariah tossed his

head in the direction of the young man behind the counter, "has been my project for the past year."

"Project?" Tess sat down at a table out on the playground and waved for the boys to come and get their meals.

"Yeah. He's been in and out of trouble since he was thirteen. I kinda took John under my wings. I got him this job, got him back into high school. He just told me he's taking the ACT test and applying to Oklahoma State. This is a kid I thought would be going to prison, not college."

Emotions swelled in her chest. Zachariah loved to help people. He loved to be totally involved in a person's life. That was great for John but not for her, not when she was trying to stand alone. She took a long sip of her iced tea while the boys came to a screeching halt next to her, plopped down in their chairs, and tore into their food.

"Hold it, young men," Zachariah said in his coach voice. "I don't think you guys need to break the world record today for eating a Happy Meal. Slow down. Savor the hamburger."

"But, Dad," Lance protested with food in his mouth. "We want—"

"And don't forget your manners," Zachariah cut in, handing his son a napkin.

"Can we stay and play after we eat?" Wesley asked, making a point to swallow his food, then wipe his mouth before speaking.

"Can we, Dad?"

Zachariah looked at Tess, a question in his eyes. He was allowing her to make the decision. Her first thought was to say no, not with all she had to do at home, but when she glanced at Wesley, she couldn't. "For twenty minutes. I have to pick up Shaun soon."

"Thanks," both boys said, jumped to their feet, and raced toward the slide.

"Were there actually two children here a moment ago?"

Tess asked, laughter in her voice. "I think they did set that world record."

"They have taken the act of bolting down their food and perfected it into an art form."

"While they're playing, I do want to talk to you about Wesley being the goalie. I'm not sure he should be."

"Why?"

"He's going to miss one day and the other team will score."

Zachariah shrugged. "That happens even to us Cimarron Devils."

"But I don't know if Wesley can take it, especially if the team loses. He'll think it's all his fault."

Zachariah captured her hand and held his cupped over hers. "I promise, Tess, it will be okay. You can't protect him all the time."

"You don't understand. Wesley shut down on me last year and I'm not sure exactly why. There's more to it than Brad leaving. I know it. I can feel it. And now, finally he's starting to come out of his self-imposed exile, maybe not exactly the way I want him to but at least he's talking. I don't want anything to jeopardize that."

"Your son has potential as a goalie. He'll only be in that position for half the game. Let him play at what he's good at. Did you see that save he made? It was good, especially for someone his age." He squeezed her hand, a grin tugging at the corners of his mouth. "I won't let anything hurt him. If he's upset, I'll make sure Wesley gets through it."

"That's not your job. It's mine." Anger generated a taut thread throughout her voice. Again Zachariah was overstepping his bounds, invading her life.

"That is my job, Tess. I'm his coach."

Tess rose. "Fine, he can play the goalie position, but remember I'm his mother. I'll take care of any emotional hurts."

Zachariah slowly stood and leaned across the table

toward her. "And who will take care of your emotional hurts?"

Stiffening, she curled her hands around the top of the chair. "I'm fine. My ex-husband can't hurt me anymore."

One of his eyebrows arched. "Is that so?"

Her fingers tightened on the plastic chair. "Yes," she said through clenched teeth.

"You could have fooled me. The way you avoid any kind of personal relationships tells me you're still running scared. What's gonna happen when you want to stop and you've pushed everyone away?"

"That's not your problem." Every muscle in her body was held so rigidly she thought she might break.

"That's what you keep telling me. I suppose one day you'll manage to get your point across."

"Wesley, it's time to go," Tess called out, trying to ignore the tension between Zachariah and her that could slice the air with a razor sharpness.

"You're so good at retreating," he murmured as Wesley ran up to them.

"Will I be able to practice extra, Mr. Smith?" her son asked, his whole attention on Zachariah.

"That's up to your mother. If she says yes, we can start tomorrow afternoon."

Wesley finally turned to Tess. "Can I, Mom? He's gonna help me be the best goalie. Mr. Smith knows *everything* about soccer."

Tess stared at Zachariah over her son's head, her lips pinched together. Wesley was forming an attachment to Zachariah that frightened her. She sensed she might not be the only one hurt if she let down her guard and allowed the man into her life. Look what happened to Wesley after Brad walked out on the family.

"Mom, can I?"

Tess blinked, breaking visual contact with Zachariah,

and glanced at her son. "Fine, if your room is cleaned. Now we'd better leave and pick up Shaun."

She didn't look at Zachariah as she walked from McDonald's, but she knew he was watching her. Why did the man want to get up close and personal? Why couldn't he just be her friend at a distance? She would be so much better off, Tess thought, but a tiny voice inside screamed, liar.

Tess poured the mineral salts under the flow of the hot water and listened to the sound as the bath filled. The scent of eucalyptus, clary sage and spearmint wafted to her, and already she felt the tension slip away as though it were cascading grains of sand in an hour glass. All day she had been looking forward to a quiet soak and some private time to relax before everyone returned home and chaos once again ruled in the household.

When the bath was ready, Tess turned off the tap and rose to get her robe. She wanted the salts to dissolve completely and the water to reach a comfortable temperature. Hurrying into her bedroom, she undressed down to her panties and slipped her robe on. As she started to leave, she spied an article of clothing sticking out from under her bed.

Puzzled, Tess knelt down and looked beneath it. She frowned as she dragged out one tennis shoe, two pairs of underwear and a sock. Bruce had found a new place to stash his "goodies." When she saw chunks of food and a bone, she swore softly and scooted further under. Wait till she got her hands on Bruce.

When she heard a whistle of appreciation, then a deep masculine voice say, "Now that's an interesting sight," Tess jerked up and hit her head on a wooden slat. Her curse could have put a sailor's to shame as she wiggled out from under the bed with her hands full of pieces of dog food and a bone, her robe riding up dangerously high, her bottom sticking up in the air.

"Sorry about surprising you, but I couldn't resist making that comment," Zachariah said from the doorway, his gaze shifting from the sight of her flushed face to the intimate and not so intimate apparel strewn about her on the floor and the bed.

Tess snatched up the two pieces of underwear and stuffed them under the mattress. "And to what do I owe this invasion of my privacy?"

"I just brought Wesley back from practicing with him."

"I thought he was eating dinner with you all," Tess said, an accusing tone in her voice. She would never have been in this predicament if she had thought there was a chance Zachariah would be bringing Wesley home. She would have made sure she was wearing enough clothing to cover her from head to toe.

"He is but he wanted to get some soldiers to use with Lance's castle and I thought since I was coming this way I would see if you and the family would like to come over this evening for a barbecue."

The question, "Why?", was out of her mouth before she had time to think about it.

He advanced into the room and held out his hand to help her to her feet. "Because you have to eat and because I like your company."

Tess grasped his hand and stood, the small confines of the room suddenly shrinking even more now that Zachariah was in it. She glanced at the rumpled sheets on her bed and an image of her and Zachariah sharing it filled her with a blazing heat like a brush fire sweeping over the landscape. She pulled free and took a step back until she came up against the night stand. Clutching the front of her robe together, she stared up at him with panic edging into her gaze.

His smile softened the hard planes of his face. "Relax, Tess. I only want you to come to dinner. Nothing more."

"It's never nothing with you, Zachariah. You want it all."

He remained where he was standing. "Will you come? The kids can have hot dogs. We'll have steaks."

She felt him crowd her as if he were in her personal space when in actuality he wasn't. She thought of her bath awaiting her and knew if she didn't take it soon the effects of the mineral salts would be ruined. And now more than ever she needed to relax and let the stress drain away.

"Fine. We'll come. Katie and Granny Kime will be home by five and Shaun by six. When do you want us to come over?" She sidestepped away from the bed and toward the door. She had to get out of this room before she didn't care that Wesley was in the house and her bath was cooling.

"As soon as Shaun comes home. We can eat out in the backyard."

"Zachariah," Wesley called out.

"In your mother's bedroom," he answered while Tess's eyes grew round.

"Zachariah? What happened to Mr. Smith?" she asked as Wesley came into the room with a box of his soldiers.

Zachariah grinned, that lopsided one that was so carefree. "Mr. Smith sounds so old, formal. Do you mind?"

She wanted to say, "What difference does it make what I think. You do what you want when you want," but instead, Tess murmured, "No."

"We'd better hit the road, Wesley, and let your mother get back to what she was doing."

Zachariah steered her son from the room but not before throwing one glance over his shoulder at her. The gleam in his eyes spoke of wants and desires. She looked away, trembling.

Tess listened to the sound of the front door closing before she released her pent up breath. She shouldn't be bothered that Wesley was calling Zachariah by his first name, but again it reminded her of how close they were becoming. Every time she turned around, she felt tied to Zachariah more and more until she was afraid she wouldn't be able to break the bonds.

When she glanced back at the bed, she realized as a picture of her and Zachariah clasped together materialized in her mind she wasn't even sure she wanted to break any bonds. A lightheadedness assailed her, and she had to remember to take a deep breath instead of holding it.

Maybe she should stop fighting this attraction and see where it led her. She shook that rebellious thought from her mind, feeling as though she were giving up on her plan to make it on her own.

As she headed for the bathroom, she recalled with determination the pain she felt first when her mother died then her father left her to be raised by her grandmother. She felt again the deep hurt she suffered when her husband abandoned her and the children. The wound of betrayal festered open and bled once more. This was what she didn't ever want to experience again. And she wouldn't if she relied only on herself, she vowed as she slipped into the soothing water.

Chapter Eight

Tess grimaced as she pulled her car up to the curb and listened to the coughing sound it made before she turned off the ignition. How was she going to make it to Oklahoma City in this piece of junk the week after next? she asked herself while Shaun threw open the doors and scrambled out of the car.

"Mommie, mommie, undo me," Katie said, wiggling her legs as she yanked at the straps on her safety seat.

With a deep sigh Tess reached into the back and unsnapped Katie, noticing for the first time she had her shoes on the wrong feet. Before Tess could say anything about that, Katie shot out of the seat and hurried after her brother.

"Hurricane Katie strikes again. I wish I had half my children's energy," Tess muttered to herself as she climbed from the car, lifting her gaze to Zachariah's front porch.

There he stood, watching her while holding Emily in his arms. An image of power and sensuality filled her vision, momentarily stunning her as if she had been instantly frozen. He had no idea the intensity he emitted, his forceful nature quietly overwhelming everything in its path, much like the hurricane she had accused Katie of being.

Tess recalled his kisses that sought to claim a part of her. She recalled his hands that sought to possess a part of her. And she recalled the emotions he sought to stir in her. Her heartbeat sped at the sight of him. All at once she regretted accepting his invitation to dinner. It was becoming impossible for her to resist his particular male charm. She didn't know how much longer she could keep him at a distance.

Slowly she walked toward him. He shifted Emily from one arm to the other, whispering in her ear, a smile tugging at the corners of his mouth. His daughter giggled and pulled on his lower lip as if to capture that smile.

"Down. Want to play," Emily said, squirming against him.

"Hold on, princess." Zachariah swung his daughter up and placed her on his shoulders. "In a minute."

Emily laughed and held onto his head. "Ride. Ride." She bounced her bottom up and down.

Zachariah descended the steps and met Tess on the walkway to his house. "The kids are out back. Where's your grandmother?"

"Enjoying a rare moment of quiet. She begged off, quickly heated up a frozen dinner, and planted herself in front of the TV."

While Emily yanked on Zachariah's hair, he looked upward as if he could see his daughter. "Probably the only sane person around."

Laughing, Tess went through the open gate and stopped just inside his fenced in yard. Shaun was tied to a tree while Lance and Wesley were playing pirates and Katie was jumping on a small trampoline, singing a silly song at a screeching level that Granny Kime probably heard four blocks away. At least her daughter had removed the shoes that were on the wrong feet.

"Definitely my grandmother was the wise one," Tess said, shaking her head.

Zachariah placed Emily on the ground, and she immediately half ran, half waddled toward Katie. "All we need to complete the picture is Bruce."

"I could always go home and get him."

"No way. If you leave, you might never come back."

His jesting words made her flinch. "I won't ever abandon my family," Tess said in a fervent voice, then walked toward her daughter. She realized she had overreacted to Zachariah's casual comment, but her response had come out before she had thought about it. It had come from a deep well of hurt.

"Katie, settle down." Tess stopped at the edge of the trampoline, aware that Zachariah was staring at her.

"Can't, Mommie. Hafta get my energy out," Katie shouted as if she were trying to be heard over her own voice.

"Well, do it quietly." Tess stood by the trampoline and watched her daughter bounce over and over. Tess knew she couldn't spend the whole evening doing this, trying to escape Zachariah, but his words earlier had renewed the old pain of abandonment that had shaped her life so much.

When Zachariah laid his hands on her shoulders, Tess realized her time was up. When he kneaded the taut muscles beneath his fingertips, she knew he wouldn't accept her walking away, that he would demand to be heard more than Katie ever would.

"I thought we knew each other well enough that I didn't have to guard everything I say."

His whispered words flowed over her neck, tingling her, reminding her of the pull he had on her. She turned then, leaning away from him so she could look up into his face.

Hurt flickered in his eyes before he killed the emotion and peered down at her with a neutral expression.

"I'm sorry, Zachariah. I was wrong to say that."

"Don't let the past rule your life, Tess. Then he really does have a lot of control over you."

She took a deep breath. "What are we having for dinner?"

He blinked as if he were trying to understand what was going on inside her mind. "Dinner?" He glanced at the barbecue. "Ah, hot dogs and steaks."

"An interesting combination. Not quite the caliber of steak and lobster."

"Too much trouble to prepare and too many questions from the kids."

"That's true. I could just hear Katie commenting about the lobsters still being alive when you cook them, the sound they make when they hit the boiling water."

"Not a pretty way to go."

Even though the air was cool his nearness generated a heat in her that rivaled the fire he was charcoaling the steaks over. The lower half of his body was thrust up against hers, his hands holding her steady, his eyes drinking her in as if he were dehydrated and needed her for life. That intensity again, Tess thought, experiencing it sweeping over her like a raging waterfall. The sounds of the children faded from her consciousness, and her whole being focused on Zachariah.

"The really smart thing to have done was hire a babysitter to stay with the kids at your place while we enjoyed a quiet dinner here." He brushed the curls from her forehead and bent to kiss it.

Not smart at all, Tess thought at the same time she hoped his mouth would move lower to cover hers. She hated the war battling inside herself, the conflict of emotions every time she was near Zachariah. Why couldn't she resist him?

"Do you think it's too late to change our plans?" he asked, pulling back slightly, his gaze fastened onto her lips.

"Yes! She swallowed hard, a tightness in her throat. She stared at the sexy curve of his mouth and couldn't say a word.

"Dad!"

Tess heard Lance's insistent voice pierce her dazed mind. She wrenched her gaze from Zachariah's mouth and looked toward his son, suddenly aware of the children playing around them.

"Dad, the fire."

Zachariah moved quickly, dumping a glass of water that he had near the grill on the fire. Smoke billowed upward. "I hope you like your steaks slightly charred."

"Slightly?" Tess asked with a shaky laugh that mirrored the trembling of her body.

"Well, maybe a little more than slightly." Zachariah flipped the steaks over to reveal a blackened surface. "Will you get the rest of the food? At least the salad and baked potatoes should be all right." He placed the hot dogs on the grill.

"Glad to." Tess welcomed the opportunity to do something other than stand there and watch Zachariah. She needed something to do to take her mind off the man. He had a way of working himself into her heart as if he meant to heal her past hurts.

By the time the dinner was ready to eat, Tess had gathered her fragile composure about her and was prepared to fend off his emotional advances. The fact that she was weak around him scared her more than she cared to admit.

"Hold it," Zachariah said as he put the plate with the meat in the middle of the table. "We're not a bunch of wild heathens." He pushed Lance's hand back and picked up the fork, spearing a steak with it. "Now, our guests first. Tess, is this okay?"

She pressed her lips together to keep from grinning as she nodded. "Perfect."

"But it's black, Mommie," Katie said.

"Just the way I like it." Tess cut into her steak and put the bite in her mouth, smiling as if it were the best piece of meat she had ever tasted.

"Your car didn't sound too good when you pulled up tonight," Zachariah said after everyone was served.

Tess took a long sip of her iced tea. "It's sputtering."

"Aren't you supposed to go to Oklahoma City next week?"

"Yeah, can you work miracles again?"

"I can do one better. I'll drive you to the city and then pick you up."

"No, that would be too much trouble." She was tempted to accept his help, but what if he wasn't around? There would come a time she had to do these things alone. In fact, she had promised herself in New Orleans the time was now.

"I don't mind. I would feel better than letting you drive that car even if I worked on it."

"I can't let you." Tess caught the tensing of his mouth, a nerve twitching in his jawline.

"Why not?"

"Because," she paused, searching her mind for a plausible reason, "because you're a busy man and it's a three hour trip one way."

"It would be fun for Emily and I to drive you down to Oklahoma City. I can take my daughter to the zoo before heading back." His gaze snared Tess's. "Are you going to deny my daughter a chance to see the animals?"

Underneath his seemingly neutral expression, she sensed a man determined to have his way. No would be unacceptable to him and she found in that instant to her also. She didn't want to drive for three hours by herself in a car ready to die at a moment's notice.

"Fine, if you're sure," Tess said, drawn to the diamond like glitter in Zachariah's eyes.

"Dad, I want to go, too," Lance broke in, his declaration pulling Zachariah's attention away from Tess.

"Me, too, Mom," Wesley chimed in.

"Sorry, kids." Zachariah held up his hand as though to ward off an attack. "It's a school day and school comes first."

"Why?" Shaun asked, wiping his mouth with the back of his hand.

"Mommie, can I have seconds?" Katie tugged on Tess's arm.

She looked down at her daughter and noticed most of her food was still untouched. "You can't until you've cleaned your plate first." Tess cut a piece of steak and ate it, taking her time chewing the meat. She listened as Zachariah tried to explain to the boys the importance of school while they argued for going on the trip to Oklahoma City.

Out of the corner of her eye, Tess saw Katie slip off the bench and take her plate toward the trash can. Just when her daughter was about to dump her food into the garbage, Tess shouted, "Katie! What are you doing?"

Her daughter turned around, one hand on her hip. "Cleaning my plate. You told me to," she said as if it were perfectly obvious what she was doing.

Everyone stopped talking and looked at Tess then Katie. For a few seconds silence reigned in the backyard.

Tess went to her daughter and took the plate from her hand. "Darling, I meant you had to finish eating everything before you can have seconds."

"Well, why didn't you say so?" Katie flounced over to the picnic table and plopped down, folding her arms across her chest, a pout forming on her lips.

Zachariah smiled at Tess, then resumed his conversation with the boys. "Sorry, you all can't go. School's too important. Besides, it will be boring driving in the car for three hours with nothing to do but talk. Now, is everyone ready for some dessert?"

Tess sat very still while the children erupted as if they were tiny volcanoes. Zachariah's comment about nothing to do but talk in the car alarmed her. Very likely she would have his full attention for three hours and he would have hers. A captive audience, she thought, realizing she wouldn't be able to get up and walk away when he probed too deeply, not when they would be going sixty-five-miles-an-hour. Somehow she doubted Emily would be enough of a diversion.

Tess closed the door on Wesley's room and walked toward the phone. Something happened at the soccer game earlier that day, the one time she hadn't gone because Katie wasn't feeling well. Tess didn't want to talk to Zachariah about this. She wanted to take care of this problem on her own, but her son wasn't talking about it.

Her heart thudded as the phone rang again then again. Her palms were sweaty while she switched the receiver to the other ear. She was almost positive that Wesley must have missed a goal. She had been afraid this would happen, that he would react negatively to what he perceived was letting the team down.

"Hello," Zachariah said, and instantly a picture of the man came to her mind.

She swallowed several times. "Zachariah, this is Tess."

"Hi, I missed you today at the game."

The sexy cadence of his voice sent her heartbeat galloping. She shifted the receiver back to the other ear and wiped her hand on her jeans, trying to ignore the thought that he had missed her. That thought excited her and she didn't want to handle the implications of that feeling.

"How's Katie? Wesley told me she was sick."

"Much better thankfully." She closed her eyes for a few seconds. Why did the very sound of his voice melt her insides? "I'm calling you about Wesley. He's despondent ever since he came home this afternoon. What happened at the game?"

"He missed a goal, but he saved several and we won. I saw him afterward and we talked. He seemed fine."

"Well, he isn't." She couldn't keep the "I told you so" tone out of her voice.

"I'll be over."

Before Tess could tell him not to come, he had hung up. She listened to the dial tone for a long moment, then slowly replaced the receiver in its cradle. She had only wanted to know what had happened so she could talk to Wesley about it. Now she had to contend with Zachariah and she wasn't emotionally prepared, not after dealing with Katie throwing up all night and morning, not after dealing with Wesley near tears all evening.

When the doorbell rang a few minutes later, Tess stiffened, drew in a fortifying breath and went to answer it. "You didn't have to come."

"I wanted to. I told you I would take care of any problems that arose because of making Wesley a goalie."

"And I told you I could take care of my son."

"I'm not doubting that, Tess, but I feel responsible for anything that happens to one of my players. I would do this for any team member." Zachariah ran his hand through his hair. "Wesley's missed some goals before so I'm not sure what's going on. May I see him?"

Tess gestured toward the hallway. "He's in his room. Shaun's spending the night at a friend's so Wesley's alone."

After he left, Tess waited a full minute before she headed back to Wesley's bedroom, intending to be a part of the discussion between Zachariah and her son. But Wesley's words stopped her in the doorway.

"At Braum's Billie's mom said the only reason you pay

attention to me and work with me is because you like my mom."

Zachariah sat on the bed next to her son, the room dim with only the light from the closet on. "That's not true."

"You don't like my mom?"

"That part is true, but not the part about paying attention to you and working with you. You're special and that has nothing to do with your mother."

A lump lodged in Tess's throat. Glad neither one had seen her, she backed away from the door and retraced her steps into the living room, a coldness embedding itself deep inside of her. This evening with Wesley was about needing reassurances that he was important in Zachariah's life. She had known that her son had a good case of hero worship, but the situation was worse than she had thought. In six weeks Zachariah had become critical to Wesley's happiness. Oh, Lord, she was in trouble. When soccer season ended in another few weeks, how was her son going to handle not seeing Zachariah on a daily basis?

How was she going to handle it?

She and Zachariah needed to talk.

She prowled the living room, glancing at her watch, expecting him to come out of her son's bedroom any moment. When thirty minutes passed and still no sign of the man, she decided to investigate again. Carefully she pushed open the door to Wesley's room a few inches and was surprised to find Zachariah sitting on her son's bed, reading him a story. Wesley's eyelids drooped closed and his head sagged to the side on his pillow.

Zachariah looked up and caught her staring at him. He smiled. The blood in her veins turned to molten lava, and she grasped the doorjamb to steady herself. He could ignite passion in her as quickly as a match tossed into a pile of dry leaves.

Carefully, so as not to awaken her son, Zachariah placed the book on the night stand and strode from the room.

Out in the hallway he took her hand without a word and led her into the living room.

"Everything's all right now," he said while gently tugging her toward the couch.

"I heard some of it. Wait till I get my hands on Billie's mother."

"No, that pleasure is all mine."

"Why?" She heard the protective ring to his words, and a part of her rejoiced, a part of her rebelled.

"I don't like what she's insinuating. I need to put a stop to her and that filthy little mind of hers before she really starts spreading rumors."

"She can't take that there might be some other child on the team as good as her son. You go right ahead and do what you must, but I'm still going to say something to her."

"Such a tigress. That's one of the things I like about you. You'll defend your family no matter what."

"You better believe that. No one will hurt my children. I can forgive a lot of things but never someone causing one of my children any pain."

Zachariah slipped his arm around her shoulders and pressed her back against his side. "Thank goodness we're on the same team."

Cradled along his length, Tess relaxed her tensed muscles and allowed herself to relish his warmth that chased away the chill of earlier. "Who's watching Emily and Lance?"

"Nora, the best neighbor a guy could have. I told her I might be a while. After all, this is Saturday night. Have any ideas what we might do now that everything's back to normal?"

Normal? Around Zachariah? Her life hadn't been normal since the day he had given her the warning. "Let's see. I haven't gotten to houseclean yet. Wanna help?"

"I'll pass. I have my own to do tomorrow. You could grow flowers in the dust I have on my furniture."

"There's always TV."

"Yeah, I'm sure there's a football game on some channel."

Tess shook her head. "Over my dead body."

He tilted up her face so she was looking into his eyes that glinted with passion. "I wouldn't want that." His voice smoked while his finger traced the outline of her mouth, slowly, mesmerizingly. "I think I can come up with something we both will enjoy."

His lips were only inches from hers. She felt his breath tingle over her hypersensitive skin and she shivered. He flattened her even more against him while his thumb tortured the column of her neck, its rough textured pad sliding down toward the pulse beat at her throat.

"Where's Katie and your grandmother?" he whispered, his head moving a fraction closer to hers.

"Who?" She couldn't seem to focus on what he was saying.

"Katie, your daughter. Granny Kime, your grandmother."

His mouth feathered over hers, and she thought she would scream when he pulled back a few inches. "Katie's asleep. Granny Kime is playing bingo until late."

"So we're alone, so to speak."

"Something like that if you call two children in the other room alone."

"In my book it's probably about the closest I'll come to being alone with you for a while."

His thumb returned to brush across her lips while his other hand glided under her T-shirt and up to cup her breast. Her eyes slid closed while delicious feelings spiraled outward from his touch. She was definitely experiencing a meltdown.

"No bra. I think I like this fashion statement," he murmured right before he crushed his lips against hers, his tongue pushing its way into her mouth much as the man had into her life, boldly, commandingly.

Wrapping her arms around his neck, she matched his passionate fire stroke for stroke. The driving possession of his mouth, the sensual probe of his tongue fired her senses and claimed a part of her locked away from others.

Their bodies meshed as he tipped her back to lie on the couch, his length covering hers. She felt his heart beat against hers as though they had melded and become one. He made slow love to her with his mouth, his hands.

Somewhere in the dark recesses of her mind she knew she needed to barricade herself against him. She couldn't. She didn't want to. She wanted this man to wipe away years of feeling self-doubt, of feeling rejected. She wanted Zachariah Smith.

She lost all sense of where she was. She became totally attuned to what he was making her feel—alive, womanly and desired.

Suddenly he stiffened. "What the hell!"

Bruce's woof echoed through Tess's disoriented mind. She saw her dog plopped on top of Zachariah. He scrambled off her while trying to fend off the Great Dane. Barking, the dog cornered him with his big paws on his shoulders, Bruce's body trapping Zachariah against the couch.

"Bruce! Get away." Tess yanked on the dog's collar to get him to move.

While Tess held the Great Dane, his eyes still trained on Zachariah, he slid as far away on the sofa as possible. "I thought you told me he was just a great big teddy bear. Couldn't harm a fly."

"He usually is. I forgot about his jealousy."

"Jealousy? A dog?" Zachariah eyed the Great Dane warily.

"Afraid so. He never liked Brad to hug me or kiss on me. He would try to break us up."

"I guess the dog isn't all bad," Zachariah muttered.

"I thought he was in Katie's bedroom. I'd better go check on her."

Before Tess could rise from the couch, her hand still clasping Bruce's collar, her daughter sauntered into the living room, rubbing her eyes. "Mommie, I want some water."

"Be right back," Tess said, dragging a reluctant dog behind her as she followed Katie from the room.

Zachariah sat on the couch, shaking his head. He could still taste Tess on his lips. He could still smell her in his nostrils. She affected his senses, making it impossible to think straight around the woman. His hands itched to hold her again. None of his desire cooled as he waited for her to return.

"Sorry about Bruce," Tess said when she reentered the living room, minus the dog. "Katie went right back to bed. I left him with her."

Zachariah could tell by the tone of Tess's voice that the spell had been broken. The cautious look was back in her eyes. She kept her distance across the room, standing near a chair, her hands gripping the back of it.

"It's been a long day, Zachariah. I didn't get much sleep last night."

He rose, wishing he didn't feel as if he had lost the clue that would unlock an important case he had been working on for months. "I'll see you Monday morning at five."

"Yes, Oklahoma City." She didn't follow him to the door but remained by the chair, her knuckles turning white.

He almost went to her, but he knew she would run. Just as he thought he was making progress, she would retreat even further into her shell. He hadn't meant to slam the door on his way out, but the sound reverberated through the stillness of the night.

Damnit. He was frustrated. He was horny.

This cinched it. Something had to be done about that dog. He would put up a fence next week while Tess was gone and surprise her when she returned. He had some friends who owed him a few favors and he was sure he could talk the neighbors into helping with paying for the lumber. Next time he found himself this close to heaven that Great Dane was going to be outside where he belonged. And there would be a next time.

Chapter Nine

Tess could see the sign for Oklahoma City ahead of her. She had spent almost three hours alone with Zachariah in the car and had survived. When he had come to pick her up, she had almost refused to go with him. At the last minute Emily's aunt had wanted her to stay over the night before and play with her daughter who was two. Tess knew that an eighteen-month-old couldn't really be a chaperon, but after what had nearly happened the other night in her living room, she was desperate.

The man was tearing down her defenses one by one, making her depend on him emotionally. First he had offered her friendship; now he offered her the chance to go much further than that into territory that in the past had left her vulnerable, wounded.

"How about breakfast before I take you to the hotel?" Zachariah asked, switching lanes on the highway in order to exit.

"That sounds fine," Tess answered absently, her attention focused on the passing scenery while her mind churned.

What if she took another risk and plunged into a relationship with Zachariah? The urge to put the past behind her was strong and growing stronger with each day she was with him. Zachariah wasn't her father. He wasn't Brad. Zachariah was forceful, sometimes overwhelming, but he always considered her feelings and listened to her. He wouldn't take over her life to the exclusion of herself.

Zachariah pulled into the parking lot of a small cafe. "Are you sure you don't need me to come pick you up Thursday?"

"Beth Linden from work is attending the conference the last two days. I can get a ride back with her," Tess answered as they entered the restaurant.

After placing their orders, he studied Tess over the rim of his coffee cup while he took several sips. "You know we should talk about Saturday night."

Tess dropped her gaze to the wooden table top. "I'm not sure I'm ready to."

"What? Talk or take the next step?"

When she looked up at him, she was reminded of the man's power and strength, etched into his hard features. She was reminded of the fact that she had almost made love to him right in her grandmother's living room with two children in the house. He obliterated any common sense she thought she had with merely his touch. "Both."

"Then let me have my say and you listen. We are attracted to each other. No amount of running away from that truth or denying it will change it. I want you, Tess. I would like us to spend some time alone together without the children."

"We are now."

His look seared through her defenses. "I have a cabin on Lake Tenkiller. I'd like to take you down there one weekend before winter sets in."

"Oh." Tess fidgeted with her fork, turning it over and over. A picture of them alone at the lake, cuddled together before a roaring fire, his arms about her, snatched the very breath from her lungs.

"Think about it while you're here. We'll resume this conversation when you return to Cimarron City."

He couldn't have gotten her attention more effectively with that statement if he had tried. For the rest of the meal and the ride to the hotel, Tess thought about nothing else but his invitation. If she committed to him, she would be opening herself and her family up to being hurt again.

At the hotel after stowing her luggage until her room was ready, Tess swung around to thank Zachariah for the ride and found him gone. She scanned the lobby and saw him standing in an alcove, staring out a large picture window with his hands clasped behind his back. Her heart skipped a beat at the sight of him so alone.

As she strode toward him, he faced her, his gaze joined with hers. Now the beat of her heart slammed against her breast in an ever increasing rate. Memories of Saturday night inundated her and her step faltered. She could again feel his hand exploring her sensitive skin; she could again taste his mouth against hers, his tongue deep inside seeking the hidden recesses within. His scent invaded the memories, sharpening them even more as she closed the distance between them.

When she came to a halt in front of him, he grasped her hands and held them between their bodies. "I know we're standing in a lobby of a busy hotel with people coming and going, but I want to kiss you, Tess. Badly."

The anticipation of that kiss created a tightening in the core of her womanhood. "What's stopping you?"

He chuckled and tugged her closer. "Nothing," he murmured and crushed her lips beneath his.

The mating of their mouths was hot, quick and hard. Before Tess had time to wind her arms around his neck, to flatten herself against him completely, he stepped back, gave her a look that curled her insides, and turned to leave.

He paused, glanced back, the silver glints in his eyes offering a promise. "We'll have that talk when you come home."

Tess sank into a nearby chair as Zachariah left the hotel. She still felt the pressure of his mouth on hers and realized she wanted much more. Dissatisfied, she brought her fingers up to graze across her lips. The thought of having to listen to lectures for the next four days made her groan. She was afraid her employer wasn't going to get his money's worth because she didn't know how she wasn't going to be thinking about Zachariah and his invitation.

As Beth turned on Oakcrest Drive, Tess rummaged around in her big purse for her keys. "I know I brought them."

"Won't someone be home?"

"Hopefully since I—" Tess latched onto her set of keys and produced them with a flourish. "I've got them." She stared out the windshield and noticed they were in her driveway. "Thanks, Beth. I really appreciate the ride. One of these days I'll be able to afford a car that actually can go more than ten miles from home."

"No problem. I enjoyed the company. The drive from Oklahoma City can be a lonely one."

"Yeah," Tess agreed, remembering her own trip to the state capital on Monday. Most of all she remembered what Zachariah had asked her to think about. Now that she was finally home, she wasn't sure she could take that next step with him. She needed to feel that she could stand alone, that she didn't have to be tied to a man to be complete. After four days she still was undecided what she should do.

Tess slipped from the car, retrieved her bag from the back seat and started for the porch. The front door flew open, and Katie raced down the steps, launching herself at Tess just as she put her piece of luggage down on the ground.

"I missed ya, Mommie."

Tess knelt in front of Katie and hugged her daughter to her. "I missed you, too, sweetheart. Talking on the phone at night just isn't the same thing as holding you."

"Pick me up." When Tess started to swung Katie up into her arms, her daughter shook her head. "No. No. Better not. I'm a big girl now. Zach says I am when I help him."

"Help him?" Suddenly Tess heard the sound of hammering and it seemed to be coming from her backyard. "Doing what, Katie?"

"We're building a fence. I hold the nails for him."

"A fence! Where?" A finely honed tension hummed through Tess's veins.

"I'll show ya." Katie took her mother's hand and began to drag her around the side of the house.

Tess barely had enough time to grab the handle of her piece of luggage before she found herself facing the gaping hole where it was obvious a gate would soon be. Anger began to simmer in her. How dare he do something like this without talking it over with her first! All at once a memory of the time Brad had brought Bruce home without consulting her and had left her to deal with the day to day upkeep of a very large dog swept into her mind. Then another memory assailed her. She would never forget when Brad had taken their lifesavings to buy a speedboat without her even knowing about it until the craft was sitting in their driveway.

Tess dropped her bag by the gaping hole and marched around the side of the house and over to where Zachariah was pounding a nail into a slat of wood. "May I ask what you think you're doing?"

He threw her a glance over his shoulder, then resumed hammering. "Putting up a fence," he mumbled around several nails in his mouth.

Tess turned to her daughter. "Sweetheart, why don't you go inside and keep Granny Kime company?"

"Don't wanna." Katie's lower lip stuck out. "I wanna stay out here wif you and Zach."

"When I get through talking with Mr. Smith, I'll give you the present I got you in Oklahoma City."

"What?"

"It's a surprise. I won't be very long."

Katie put her thumb in her mouth and stared up at her mother then at Zachariah for a long moment. "Okay." She whirled and ran for the house.

"So we're back to Mr. Smith," Zachariah said after removing the nails from his mouth and carefully placing his hammer on the ground next to the pile of wooden slats.

"Who gave you the right to come into my backyard and put up a fence?"

"Your grandmother."

Tess blinked, for some reason not expecting that answer. "Why?"

"Because Bruce needed a place to stay."

Tension whipped down the length of her body. She again experienced the feeling of being circumvented, of her wishes being ignored. "I didn't realize Bruce was your concern. It wasn't your place to take matters into your own hands."

"Look, Tess. I only wanted to help you out. Some of my buddies have been helping me put up the fence. I'd hope to surprise you and have it completed by the time you got home, but Robert and Ned were called away on an emergency this afternoon."

"You waited until the first time I was out of town and then you went behind my back. Maybe I like things just the way they are."

"Yeah, that's your problem. You won't take a risk."

"This isn't about taking a risk." Tess waved her hand toward the unfinished fence. "This is about you doing something supposedly for me and yet you weren't really sure I wanted it or you would have asked me. Brad used to do that. According to him I wanted a Great Dane. Then I wanted a speedboat so he could go to the lake every weekend and leave me alone with the children and the dog." Her voice rose with her anger. All the times Brad had not consulted her swamped her with feelings she thought she had been slowly working through.

"It always comes back to Brad. Are you going to let that man rule your life forever?"

Tess sucked in a deep breath and held it until her lungs ached. "I can't afford a fence," she said, refusing to answer his question.

His eyes narrowed for a few seconds as though debating whether to pursue the subject of Brad or not. "I got the neighbors to pitch in with the cost of the lumber so it won't be much. You can pay me back later when you have the money."

"You've overstepped your bounds as my friend."

"I thought we were more than friends. What did you think was happening?"

"I don't need your help in taking care of *my* dog," she said in a forceful tone, realizing she was ignoring his comment about their developing relationship. She couldn't answer him on that; she couldn't think about that at the moment.

He took a step closer to her. "Listen, you told me you didn't like putting Bruce on a rope when he went outside. Now you don't have to."

"What else have you decided about my family since I've

been gone? Have you mapped out Wesley's career as a soccer player? Will it be more than insisting he play goalie?"

"This has nothing to do with Wesley."

"Doesn't it? You're always there ready to help, ready to take over. Will I have a say in anything having to do with my children?"

Anger hardened the planes of his face, a nerve jerked in his jaw. "Tess, you're blowing this all out of proportion."

"Am I?" She raised one brow in a mocking gesture, intense feelings snapping her body taut.

"What are you really afraid of? What I asked you to think about? Becoming intimate with me? What?" He started to reach for her but she backed away. With teeth clenched, he fisted his hands at his sides and inhaled in a deep breath.

She watched him struggle to gain control but she didn't care. Days of contending with an internal clash played havoc with her raw emotions. She felt sapped of energy, tired of not knowing what to do, of seesawing between her vow to herself and her blossoming feelings concerning Zachariah. Her life wasn't hers any longer. She felt like a puppet with someone else pulling the strings.

"Let's talk some place less public," he said, a neutral expression descending over his features.

"Why should we? You chose to go behind my back and decide for me what was best," she goaded, upset that he could get a grip on his emotions while inside she shredded, piece by piece.

This time he moved with a lightning quick speed and grabbed her upper arms. He yanked her close against his body. "I'll take this damn fence down if that's what you want."

The words exploded from his mouth, bathing her in his hot fury. She twisted against him, but his grip only strengthened. "Yes, that's what I want."

"Stop it. Stop it," Wesley shouted from behind Tess.

Time paused for a few seconds as her son's plea penetrated her anger. Zachariah released her and she stumbled backward. When she spun toward Wesley, she saw the tears streaming down his face, the hurt etched into his expression as though it had come from the depths of his soul. But for the life of her, her parched throat captured her words and held them tightly inside.

"Why are you two fighting? It's just like Dad and you," her son said, then spun about and ran from the backyard.

Wesley's flight set her in motion. She raced after her son, her heart pounding as quickly as her feet. She couldn't think beyond the fact she had to reach him, hold him and explain to him.

He kept running across the front yard and toward the street. Tess saw the car coming as though it were moving in slow motion, as though the scene were painted in tones of gray, surrealistic, nightmarish. Yards away from Wesley all she could do was shout for him to stop. He didn't for several more feet, then suddenly he came to a halt in the middle of the street, as if he finally realized something was wrong, and whirled about as the car slammed into his body, tossing him up into the air and onto the hood. The thud reverberated through her mind, replaying continuously like a stuck record on a stereo.

Tess screamed, over and over.

The screech of the tires coalesced with her outcries to blend into one horrendous sound. Tess was a few feet away when her son rolled from the hood and struck the pavement near the left front tire.

"Oh, my God. Oh, my God," she said as she reached Wesley, lying in the street, his right leg bent at an odd angle, his eyes closed, his chest rising and falling rapidly with shallow breaths.

Mustn't move him, she thought while frantically trying to remember her first aid course in high school. But she desperately wanted to scoop him up into her arms and absorb all his pain into her own body. She desperately wanted to take back the past ten minutes and redo the terrible scene all over. And most of all she desperately wanted to change places with her son. He should never have to suffer because of her.

"This should be me. Never Wesley. Not my baby," she cried as she felt his thready pulse beat beneath her fingertips at his neck. She brushed the wet tracks from her son's cheeks while her own tears flowed down her face. Around her she heard voices, urgent ones, upset ones, but she didn't have time to listen. She must help Wesley.

Strong hands clasped her arms and began to lift her away from her son. "No!" She tried to wrench free, but the strength of the grip only increased. "I have to help him."

"Tess, let me," Zachariah said in a voice demanding she obey.

"No, you've helped enough." She had an overriding urge to hold her son, to cling to him. She was so afraid it would be the last time.

Zachariah knelt down next to her. "Listen, Tess." He waited until she looked up into his face. "I've been trained in emergency care."

His soothing voice, with a hint of gravity, pierced through the haze that clouded her mind. Wesley lay so still, his skin clammy to the touch. Panic began to take hold and weave its way through her as she acknowledged she might lose her son. "I'm his mother. He needs me."

"Tess." Zachariah's fingers dug into her upper arms as he dragged her toward him and away from Wesley. "Someone has called for an ambulance, but I want to check him."

She stared into Zachariah's storm dark eyes, then scooted a few inches away so that he could tend to Wesley. Her heart felt as if it were breaking into a thousand pieces as she watched through the sheen of her tears as Zachariah examined her son. She saw the pool of blood on the pavement where his head had hit and bit her lower lips until she tasted her own. She heard in the distance the ambulance's siren and the sound brought home to her the fragility of the situation. Would it arrive in time? Would she hold Wesley again in her arms?

"Here's some coffee," Zachariah said when he reentered the hospital waiting room and placed a Styrofoam cup into Tess's hand.

Automatically, without a thought, Tess lifted the hot drink to her mouth and sipped. She winced and put the cup on the table next to her chair. "I don't like coffee."

"I know but I thought you might need the stimulant."

"I couldn't sleep if my life depended—" Her words faded into the silence. Her son was this very moment on an operating table fighting for his life and there was nothing she could do but sit and pray. And wait.

Tears, ever quick to return, sprang into her eyes. She jumped to her feet and began to pace, thankful that no one else was in the room. She was afraid at any moment she would fall apart.

"Tess, I called your grandmother to check on Shaun and Katie. They are finally in bed asleep."

Zachariah's words registered in her thoughts, but their meaning was fleeting as if an idea just within grasp kept teasing her then fading away into the blankness of her mind. She couldn't concentrate long on anything except putting one foot in front of the other.

Humpty Dumpty sat on a wall.
Humpty Dumpty had a great fall;
All the King's horses and all the King's men
Couldn't put Humpty Dumpty together again.

One of Katie's favorite nursery rhymes played over and

over in Tess's numbed mind as she walked from one end of the small waiting room to the other. She felt the cracks in her facade as if she had fallen from a high place. If Wesley didn't make it, she didn't know if she would be able to pull herself together for her other two children.

She glanced at her watch. "How long is it going to take? They've been working on him for two hours." Two hours of hell, she thought as she swiped at the tears rolling down her cheeks.

"They had to relieve the pressure on his brain, set his leg. That takes time, Tess. He'll be all right."

All right? "Do you know something I don't know?" Shudder after shudder rippled down the length of her. She would never forget how her son had looked as the paramedics placed him in the ambulance. Like a broken doll.

Zachariah covered the distance between them in three long strides and drew her into his arms. For several heartbeats, she allowed him to hold her, to comfort her, but then the scene in the backyard rushed into her mind with all the guilt she was trying to keep at bay. Their fight was the reason Wesley was on an operating table right now. She tried to pull free, but Zachariah only tightened his arms about her.

"Let me help. What can I do for you?" Zachariah asked, his hand rubbing up and down her back.

This time when she jerked away, he let her go. "Nothing. You've done more than enough." The words came out in an accusing tone as she backed away. If she wasn't hurting so much herself, she might have responded to the look of pain that flashed into his eyes. But she couldn't; she didn't have it in her. "You don't need to stay."

"I am."

"I'd rather you leave."

"I'm not, Tess."

"I want to be alone."

"That's the worse thing you can be right now."

"Don't you dare tell me what's good or bad for me. That's one of the reasons we are here right now."

He flinched as if she had slapped him.

"I want to be alone, Zachariah." She pronounced the sentence slowly and loudly.

He remained standing in front of her, determination slowly covering up the sadness in his eyes.

"What do I have to do to make you leave me alone?"

He started to say something but instead clamped his jaw tightly together. With a step back he positioned himself near the doorway.

Couldn't put Tess together again.

The cracks in her facade were fissures now, wide and deep, clear to her soul. She didn't want him to see her come apart. "If you won't go, I will."

He gave her one last, long look, then pivoted and left. The quiet in the waiting room crashed down on her and the fragile hold she had on her emotions shattered. Hugging her arms to her, she fell into a nearby chair and sobbed, rocking back and forth to stem the flow of pain that coursed through her body like a river out of control. Nothing took the feelings of hurt and helplessness away—not the silence, not the release of her tears, not the absence of Zachariah.

"Mrs. Morgan."

She heard her name as thought it were spoken through a vacuum. She glanced up and saw the teary blur of the surgeon in his green scrubs standing in the doorway. "Is my son all right?"

Chapter Ten

Tess stared at the amount owed at the bottom of the hospital bill, not sure where in the world she would come up with the money. Thank goodness at least her son would be all right in time. After spending two weeks in the Memorial Medical Center, Wesley would be going home today with a cast on his leg and his head shaved the only visible signs of his accident.

Sighing deeply, she clutched the piece of paper in her hand and left the cashier's office for her son's room. With leadened steps she headed down the corridor. She was so tired and mentally exhausted after spending endless hours waiting during Wesley's operation, during his recovery. She had spent endless hours at his bedside, reassuring herself that her son would make it. She had spent endless hours berating herself for the scene in the backyard the day of his accident.

As she approached her son's hospital room, she saw Zachariah leaving it. She hadn't seen him in the two weeks since she had asked him to leave her alone while Wesley was in the operating room. Somehow Zachariah always knew when she was away from her son and managed to pay him a visit during that time.

Zachariah stopped in the hallway, his gaze locked with hers. Tall, powerful, he wore his uniform as though he were capable of taking care of anything. And he was, she thought, her heart tripling its rate at the sight of him, his expression unreadable.

"We need to talk," Zachariah said and started forward, gesturing for her to enter the waiting room behind her.

When she faced him, she noticed the tensed set of his shoulders, the clench of his jaw, the same tired look in his eyes as she felt. Since the accident she hadn't thought she could deal with him and the emotions he generated in her, not with all she had to handle the past two weeks. Now though, she knew she would have to and she didn't know if she was mentally prepared. Confusion reigned inside her whenever she was with Zachariah Smith and that fact hadn't changed in the time since she had last seen him.

"What's that? The bill?" Zachariah pointed at the piece of paper still clasped in her hand.

She nodded.

"I want to pay it. I'm to blame for Wesley being in the hospital."

"No," Tess said quickly, her grip on the paper tightening.

He paced away from her, putting the length of the waiting room between them. When he pivoted, he raked his hand through his hair repeatedly. "Damnit, Tess. I need to pay the bill. If I hadn't put up that fence, he wouldn't be lying in that hospital bed right now."

"Wesley's my responsibility, not yours," Tess said, intending to explain he wasn't to blame but herself. She should never have caused the scene in the backyard in the first place.

Before Tess could formulate the words of explanation, Zachariah said in a tight voice, "You're too damn proud. You just can't accept help, can you? There's nothing wrong with admitting that you might need someone."

The frigid shards in his eyes chilled her, making her forget everything she was going to say. All of a sudden her anger matched his. "No." To make her point, Tess took the bill and stuffed it deep into her purse. She would not be steamrolled into doing something she didn't want to do.

His gaze narrowed, his jaw a harsh, forbidden line. "It's over between us, Tess. And don't kid yourself. We had something going." He combed his fingers through his hair and kneaded the corded muscles of his neck. "I'll tear down that fence this weekend. After that you won't have to see me again."

"What about Wesley? He worships you." Panic crept into her voice while she frantically tried to remain calm. She knew in her heart she owed him an apology for the way she had treated him in the waiting room the night Wesley had been operated on, but she couldn't stop the rejected feelings from her past engulfing her now.

"I'll still be Wesley's soccer coach next spring and he'll still be Lance's friend. He'll always be welcomed at my house."

"But not his mother?" She laid her hand over her chest as though that would ease the crushing pain spreading outward to encompass her whole body.

Zachariah shook his head. "I need more than your kind of friendship. I need someone who will trust me, let me truly be a part of her life. I need a commitment, a relationship, a partnership, fifty-fifty. I thought this could work. I was wrong."

"So you're going to walk away?" Just like Brad, just like her father, Tess added silently, taking in one deep breath after another but nothing seemed to help the hurt.

"Yes. I just wish to God you needed me. Once—you really needed me." Zachariah strode toward the door. "Good-bye, Tess."

The finality of those words sliced through all of Tess's fragile defenses she had painstakingly erected to keep herself from feeling any pain. She hugged her arms to her as she watched him punch the down button for the elevator. When he got on it, he looked up at her and their gazes connected. For a heartbeat, she could have sworn his gray eyes were glazed with a deep hurt, but before she could discern for sure what she saw, he masked his expression and glanced away. The doors swished closed.

Suddenly Tess half ran, half walked toward the bank of elevators, tears blurring her vision. She had to stop him. She had to tell him—what? She didn't know what to say to him. Confusion mixed with the feeling of betrayal to mangle her emotions. She turned away, wanting to double over and curl into a tight ball.

Couldn't put Tess together again.

She leaned against the wall and held herself. "I won't cry," she murmured over and over, but her tears flowed down her cheeks unchecked.

He had been right. She didn't know how to accept help. She was afraid to become indebted to someone. She had been forced to accept her grandmother's assistance because of the children. She had hated to admit she couldn't make it on her own when she had moved from New Orleans. Every time she had started to depend on someone, that person had left, first her mother when she had died, then her father and finally Brad.

Tess wiped at the tears that still ran down her face. She had to compose herself before she went in to see Wesley to take him home. She couldn't upset her son again—not after the scene she had created in the backyard. Her fear of not being in total control of her relationship with Zachariah had driven her—and still did. But the past two weeks she had learned what not being in control of a situation meant. Life couldn't be completely planned no matter how hard she tried.

No matter how much she wanted to be calm and together for her son, the hurt wouldn't let go. It burrowed deep into her heart, constricting her throat, burning her lungs. Zachariah was gone. That realization struck her with the force of a sledgehammer, sending pain coursing through her body.

She loved him.

And it was too late.

She squeezed her eyes closed to silence the tears, but a lone one slipped from beneath her lashes and streaked down her cheek. She had come to Cimarron City determined to stand on her own two feet, to make it alone. Now she truly was alone and it hurt like a wound that wouldn't heal.

Sucking in shallow breaths, she fought for control. Wesley needed her. She had to mend her son's pain before she could deal with hers. Placing the flat of her hand on the door into his room, she pushed her way inside, praying he didn't sense anything was wrong.

"Mom. Look what Zachariah brought me!" Her son held up a Star Wars figure. "It's one of the Emperor's guards. Isn't it neat?"

Her throat contracted. She nodded, not daring to speak, her emotions still too brittle.

"This makes my twelfth figure. I'm gonna have the best collection ever. Better than Jimmy's and Willie's." Wesley beamed from ear to ear while he fingered the plastic man garbed in blood red.

Tess smiled at her son, the corners of her mouth trembling. "Well, partner, are you ready to break out of this joint?"

"You betcha. I get to ride in a wheelchair. The nurse said so."

"Sounds like a plan to me. Everyone can't wait for you to get home."

"Did you get to see," her son paused, dropping his gaze to stare at the white sheet covering his lower body, "Zachariah before he left?"

Tess looked away, so afraid her raw emotions shone in her eyes. "Yeah."

"Did—did you two—you two make up?" Wesley twisted the sheet into a wad.

Tess drew in a sharp breath and held it until she thought her lungs would explode. This wasn't the place or the time that she had wanted to discuss what had happened in the backyard, but she saw the worried expression in her son's gaze when he lifted it toward her. "We spoke."

"Then he'll be coming over?"

She turned away, pulled the chair close to the bed, and sat. "Wesley, it's more complicated than that."

"You didn't make up." Tears welled up in her son's eyes, his bottom lip quivering. "It's all my fault. He's gone because of me."

Tess grasped his hands and held them. "No. Never because of you."

"You were fighting just like Dad and you right before Dad left. I heard you the night before. You were fighting about me." Tears spilled from his eyes, splashing onto their clasped hands. "I heard you and Zachariah talking about me. I'm the reason you fought."

For a few seconds Tess didn't understand then she remembered saying Wesley's name in the course of the fight. "We were arguing about the fence, honey. Not you."

He sniffed several times, but he continued to cry, his shoulders hunched forward. "Why did Dad leave us? What did I do wrong?"

Quickly Tess gathered her son into her arms, pressing his head to her chest as she stroked him. "You did *nothing* wrong. Your father thought I did something wrong, not you. He's the one losing out on being with us. You, Shaun, Katie and I are the lucky ones. We have each other. He doesn't have anyone now." She didn't think it was possible for her chest to feel such intense pressure. It was hard to breathe. It was hard to feel anything but the ache her son's words produced.

"Do you think he'll come back?"

"I don't know, sweetheart." She pulled back and cupped her son's face in her hands, her thumbs wiping his tears away while she fought her own. She had to be strong for Wesley. "You have me, and no matter what, that will never change." Her throat closed around each word as she spoke while her own eyes watered.

"I love you, Mom."

"And I love you, hon. Never doubt that." She drew him against her and wrapped her arms about him as if that would convey her feelings to her son.

"You will make up with Zachariah," Wesley mumbled against her chest, confidence in his voice.

And in that moment Tess realized her son was right. At least she knew she would try to make up with Zachariah. The big question was: would he want to make up with her? She hoped so because she wasn't sure she could or wanted to make it anymore on her own.

Tess stared out the kitchen window over the sink at Zachariah taking down the fence. He yanked off a wooden slat and tossed it to the ground, his action full of purpose, full of anger. She had thought in the hospital the last time she had seen him dressed in his uniform that he looked powerful, capable of taking care of anything. But it had nothing to do with his uniform, she realized as she watched him work, his body clad in black jeans and T-shirt. Zachariah had made her feel secure, safe, not just physically but emotionally. He had weaved his way into her life until he had become entwined with her as tightly the threads of a piece of cotton material.

It had been three days since Wesley had come home from the hospital and with each day that had passed Tess's conviction had grown stronger. She knew what she wanted, she needed. Zachariah Smith. The emptiness she had felt after he had walked away from her had left a hollowness that she didn't think she could fill with friends, work, activities.

She must do something now or she would lose him. But what if he rejected her? Memories of Brad and her father wormed their way into her thoughts, but she instantly shoved them away. That was the past. This was the present—and her future, if she could convince Zachariah to give her another chance.

But she remembered the hurt she had glimpsed in his eyes as the elevator had closed and she didn't know if he would allow her into his heart again. He had every right to turn away from her. She had been wrong, so very wrong. She wasn't a risk taker, but she would do what she needed to get him back.

Inhaling a fortifying breath, she walked to the back door and placed her hand on the knob. Now or never, she thought and stepped out onto the small porch. Crisp, fall air cooled her heated cheeks as she gripped the railing.

"Zachariah, I need to see you."

Hammer in hand, he slowly turned and his cold look skewered her, sending frozen fragments through her body. "What about?"

"I have some coffee brewing. Come inside and have a cup with me."

"You don't drink coffee."

"I know. I made it for you."

"Why?"

"To have with the cinnamon rolls I baked. Please." Her

hands ached from gripping the railing so tightly. Not one bit of coldness melted in his eyes.

"Five minutes. I still have a lot of work to do." He threw the hammer down by the stack of wooden slats.

"That's what I want to talk to you about," she said as he passed her to go into the kitchen.

Just inside the doorway he spun about. "What?" Impatience sounded in his voice.

"I want to keep the fence."

He didn't say anything for a full minute, his regard now void of any expression. Then all of a sudden anger replaced his blank look, carving a frown into his face. "Lady, make up your mind."

"I have. I want the fence. You were right about Bruce."

The hardened line of his jaw jerked. His eyes drilled into her with a relentless fury. "It doesn't make any difference now."

"I was wrong, Zachariah. About a lot of things."

"So, what do you want me to say? Great. We'll pick things up where we left off before Wesley's accident."

"Yes—no. I know we need to talk about what happened. I need to explain. Please sit." She gestured toward the kitchen table.

He looked at where she pointed then back at her. "It won't change anything." He didn't budge but continued to stare at her with that cutting regard.

Pain sliced through her like a machate through thick vines. "I'm not too proud that I won't beg."

"Beg?"

"You told me at the hospital that I was too proud. I may have been then. I'm not now. I learn from my mistakes and this is too important to me."

He crossed the kitchen in two strides and sat at the table, his expression totally closed off to her. For a few seconds Tess stood immobile, listening to the silence of the house. Thankfully everyone was gone this afternoon and she wouldn't have an audience while she pleaded her case with Zachariah.

"Would you like some coffee? A cinnamon roll?" she asked, suddenly needing something to do as she gathered her courage.

"Fine," he clipped out between clenched teeth.

She busied herself taking the rolls out of the oven and putting several on a plate for him. Then she poured him a cup of coffee and placed the drink and pastry in front of him. When she took the seat across from him, she still wasn't sure how to begin explaining her feelings. She had never been good at that. She had always guarded how she felt very close to her heart.

"I can help you finish putting up the fence. There isn't much left to do," she said, watching him take a bite of a cinnamon roll, then several sips of his coffee. "That is if you'll agree to finish the fence."

"I'd planned to spend a few hours taking it down, so I guess I can take that time to complete it instead." His gaze lifted to seize hers in a long, searching look. "Why, Tess? What's this about?"

"My past, the past you accused me of not being able to let go."

His brow wrinkled, his eyes becoming pinpoints. "Are you telling me you have?"

"I hope so." She glanced away, his intense gaze stripping away her nerve. "I don't know how to begin, Zachariah. I'm not very good with words."

"Oh, I'd say you can get your point across. In the hospital when Wesley was being operating on, you made yourself crystal clear to me. You wanted nothing to do with me beyond that of an acquaintance."

She swung her regard back to his face and saw the pain in his eyes before he veiled his expression. "This's not fair. You shouldn't hold me responsible for what I said or did that night."

"I didn't at first until I saw you again in the hospital corridor and you still couldn't allow me to help you. That's when I knew it was time to move on. I'll beat my head against the wall only so long."

His voice sounded so detached as he spoke that Tess's heart skipped a beat, then thudded slowly. "For years I've been afraid of rejection. After my husband left me, my motto became reject before you are rejected," she said with a shaky laugh. "I kept people at a distance. I was determined to go it alone. When I had to accept my grandmother's help because of the children, I thought I had failed somehow. So I was even more determined not to accept anyone else's help when I moved to Cimarron City. I thought I had something to prove to myself."

Zachariah brought his mug to his lips and took a swallow of the coffee, his eyes bound to hers. "So you think you're ready to accept help? Is that what this fence thing proves?"

The coldness in his question made her breath catch. "And this." She reached into her jeans pocket, withdrew a piece of paper and slid it across to him.

He read it. "The hospital bill?"

"Yeah. The insurance company is paying eighty percent, but that still leaves twenty for me. You wanted to help me pay for Wesley's accident. I'm accepting your offer. Whatever you want to pay is fine with me."

"Even all of it?"

She nodded.

Surprise flickered into his gaze. He whistled. "The fence *and* the bill."

"I'm serious." She gripped the edge of the chair she was sitting in. "I was wrong about so many things, especially you and I."

He swallowed hard, then slowly shook his head. "I just can't take the chance. When Wesley had the accident that was a time for you and I to grow closer. You needed someone to lean on and you pushed me away. I can't tell you how much that hurt."

Her fingers dug into the wood of the chair. She felt his pain and knew she was losing him. "I love you, Zachariah."

He didn't respond to her declaration. He stared at the table in front of him.

Panic rose to choke her throat. She felt it tightening, cutting off her breath. She had to do something to convince him, something bold, a risk. Standing on shaky legs, she walked around the table and sat in his lap, putting her arms around his neck before he rejected her.

His gaze riveted to hers. "What the hell?"

"This is called seduction, Mr. Smith. It's obvious you don't believe my words when I say them so I'll show you that I love you. If you haven't figured it out by now, saying those words doesn't come easily to a woman who doesn't give herself away much, who in the past has had them thrown back into her face."

Tess cupped her hands along his jawline and brought her mouth down hard on his. It took only a few seconds for him to decide to part his lips enough to allow her tongue to explore inside. His taste was like nectar; his scent was like an aphrodisiac, inflaming her body. She melted against him, wanting to become a part of him. His arms came up to encircle her and press her even closer.

"Where is everyone?" he asked, his voice husky with desire.

"Gone. Even Wesley. Granny Kime took him and Katie to a movie."

"And Bruce?" Zachariah nibbled a path to her earlobe and feasted on it.

She snuggled into his chest, her bottom squirming in his lap. "Corralled in the boys' bedroom."

"Then we are really alone?"

She nodded, unable to say another word while his mouth devoured her sensitive earlobe.

Suddenly he stopped kissing her and held her away. "For how long?"

She blinked several times, trying to bring her rioting senses under control long enough to answer him. "An hour."

"Not long enough. When we make love, Tess Morgan, I want to spend all day and night, exploring every inch of your body, kissing every inch of your body."

The flames in his eyes scorched her. "When we make love?" she murmured in a barely audible voice, every inch of that body on fire.

He took her face within his large hands. "We're gonna do this proper. Will you marry me? Soon? Because if you don't, I don't know how long I can control myself."

"Yes." Tears misted in her eyes.

He breathed deeply. "God, I don't know if I can wait. You're one sexy lady."

"It's the cinnamon. It's an aphrodisiac. I made the rolls deliberately."

He tossed back his head and laughed. "You didn't have to go to all that trouble. Just one look at you does it every time or hadn't you figured that out by now?"

"This is new for me. I've never felt so—cherished."

"And loved. Don't forget that, Tess. I love you with or without your cinnamon."